ONCE UPON A LIE

A Fitzjohn Mystery

JILL PATERSON

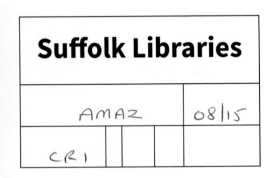
Once Upon A Lie

ISBN 978-0-9873955-4-2

Publisher: J. Henderson, Canberra, Australia

Cover design: Renee Barratt http://www.thecovercounts.com

For Emily

Acknowledgements

Many thanks to my dear friend Anna Mullins for her unflagging support. Thank you also to my sister, Val, for her editing skills, and Melissa and John for their help and advice on the environs of Sydney. Also, once again, a special thank you to Catherine Hammond for her help and advice.

ONCE UPON A LIE

{CHAPTER 1}

E sme's eyelids flew open, her body tensed and her arthritic joints twinged as the scraping sound came again from the room above. She turned her head slightly to look at the clock on the bedside table, its numbers illuminated in the darkened room. Twenty-three minutes past two. A myriad of frenzied thoughts ran through Esme's mind. She knew every creak and squeak in the old house. They were many and varied, but this was different. Shivering despite the warmth of the March night, Esme strained to hear through the pulsating in her ears. Moments passed before it came again, and when it did, she stiffened. 'This is ridiculous,' she muttered, turning over, 'get a grip on yourself, girl.' Esme closed her eyes and let her thoughts go back to the previous evening when her nephew, Michael, had dropped by. Not unusual in itself. He often called in to check on her. But last night was different. This time it was not a social call, but a request that she allow him to rummage through the rooms upstairs; in particular, the one his sister, Claudia, had used as a study before her untimely death. Esme sighed. How long ago was that? A year or more and still Michael insisted that foul play was involved. Why did he persist?

Barely had that thought crossed Esme's mind when the floorboards above creaked again. There is someone up there. Unless, of course, Michael opened the window while he was up there and that wretched possum got in. Esme rose from her bed, put her dressing gown on, and slipped her feet into a pair of faded pink slippers. As she did so, her eyes fell upon her walking cane hooked over the bed head. She loathed using the thing, refusing to accept that at eighty-one it helped steady her. But in this case, it could have other uses, she thought, running her fingers over the carved metal handle. Picking it up, and gingerly peering out of the bedroom door, she felt her way along the passage. Faltering as the living room clock chimed the half hour, Esme continued on to the foot of the staircase where she hesitated. She had rarely been upstairs since her fall two years ago. Only Claudia's study had seen any use since that time. Esme grabbed the banister and sighing, made her slow ascent. Minutes passed before she reached the landing to find it bathed in moonlight from the window at the end. Trying to still her panic, she moved into the shadows and peered towards the study, its door ajar. Had Michael forgotten to close the door? If not, who… With her heart pounding in her tiny frame, Esme edged along the passage, her trembling hand gripping the middle of her walking cane. It was then the door moved inward and a figure, silhouetted in the moonlight, stepped out in front of her. Esme gasped and raised her cane. It was the last thing she remembered.

{CHAPTER 2}

Summonsed back from leave, Detective Chief Inspector Alistair Fitzjohn settled himself comfortably into the Silver Cab as it sped off through the streets of Birchgrove toward Sydney's CBD, and Day Street Police Station. His thoughts traversed the last few weeks, encapsulating his journey back to York in England at the behest of his sister Meg. He hated to admit it, but she had been right. The journey to the places where he and his late wife Edith spent their youth had brought him a sense of peace at last, lifting him out of the quagmire he had been in for the past eighteen months.

As the cab pulled up in front of the station, Fitzjohn adjusted his wire-framed glasses and grabbed his briefcase. As he did so, he wondered what was in store for him now that Grieg had been elevated to Acting Chief Superintendent. With his once rotund shape somewhat diminished by an activity-packed holiday, Fitzjohn paid the driver, climbed out of the taxi, and made his way inside, where the familiar sights and sounds gave rise to a feeling of contentment. The acknowledgement of those around him of his return as he walked through the station added to his pleasure. When Betts, his tall, ginger-haired Sergeant appeared, Fitzjohn's return to duty was complete, and with a wide smile, he took the young officer's outstretched hand.

'Sir. You're looking well.'

Fitzjohn looked down at his dark blue suit that hung unusually loose. 'The result of spending a month on holiday with my sister, and being persuaded into adopting her healthy eating regime. I dare say I'll have to pay my tailor a visit.' They continued on through the station toward Fitzjohn's office.

'Do you have any idea why I've been called back from leave, Betts?'

'Yes. All hell broke loose early this morning, sir, when Chief Superintendent Grieg was asked to provide assistance in a suspicious death over at Rushcutters Bay.'

Fitzjohn stopped suddenly, his hand dropping from his office door handle. 'Did I hear you correctly? Grieg's no longer *Acting* Chief Superintendent?'

'No, sir, he's the Chief.'

Fitzjohn ran his hand over the few remaining wisps of hair on top of his head as the frustration at not being able to voice his opinion of Grieg to his Sergeant, got the better of him. 'How could such a thing happen? Before I left, I really thought that, in the end, commonsense would prevail, but it seems not.' Realising this was a purely rhetorical statement, Betts did not reply as they walked into Fitzjohn's office. While Fitzjohn put his briefcase on his desk and commenced removing his papers, Betts opened the blinds.

'So, what's this about a suspicious death?' asked Fitzjohn, brushing the dust from his chair before sitting down.

'Well, it seems...'

At that moment, loud voices sounded outside Fitzjohn's office before the door burst open and Chief Superintendent Grieg walked into the room, his imposing, heavy-set frame lending an air of dominance. 'Fitzjohn.' Fitzjohn got slowly to his feet while Grieg's beady brown eyes glared at Betts, who headed for the door. 'Don't go Detective Sergeant Betts.' said Grieg. 'I take it you've told Detective Chief Inspector Fitzjohn of the situation.'

'I was just about to, sir.'

'Ah, well, in that case let me enlighten you, Fitzjohn. A body was found early this morning at a marina in Rushcutters Bay. The victim was one of the owners of an electronics business there. Rossi & Prentice Yachting Electronics Pty Ltd. The Kings Cross LAC is short-staffed and has requested our assistance, so I'm seconding you.'

'For how long, sir?' asked Fitzjohn, frowning.

'For as long as it takes.' Grieg's pudgy face smirked. 'And judging by the length of time you took on your last case, that may be some time.' Fitzjohn ignored the remark, detecting Grieg's pleasure at imparting this news that would ensure his absence from the station. 'Kings Cross will provide you with an incident room and whatever else you require, so...'

'So, I have no need to be here.' Unable to contain his indignation, Fitzjohn gathered his papers, putting them back into his briefcase before slamming it shut. 'We'll be off, then.'

'Oh, I mustn't have made myself clear. Detective Sergeant Betts won't be accompanying you,' said Grieg with a bemused smile. 'He has other duties to attend to.'

Was it Fitzjohn's newfound peace, knowing he no longer needed his work as a coping mechanism since Edith's death, or was it his revulsion for Grieg, that made him throw caution to the wind and reply, 'In that case, I'll continue my annual leave.' Fitzjohn grabbed his briefcase and started toward the door.

'That would be a grave mistake, Fitzjohn.'

Fitzjohn stopped and glared at Grieg. 'Mistake or not, *Chief* Superintendent, I'll need Betts if I'm going to take on this case.'

Grieg's face reddened. 'You'll regret this, Fitzjohn. Mark my words.'

As the door slammed behind Grieg, Fitzjohn turned to Betts. 'I'm sorry you had to witness that, Betts.'

'Did I miss something? What happened there, sir?'

'Nothing that concerns you, Betts.' Fitzjohn smiled to himself, aware that his knowledge of Grieg's infidelity gave him the edge he needed in dealing with the now, Chief Superintendent. Chuckling to himself he said, 'Let's be on our way, shall we?'

{CHAPTER 3}

F itzjohn and Betts arrived on New Beach Road in Rushcutters Bay twenty minutes later. Bordered by tall deciduous trees, the roadway gave the impression of coolness in the early morning heat. In stark contrast, the predominantly white facades of the dwellings facing the Bay and clinging precariously to the hillside, glared in the morning sun. Continuing past the Cruising Yacht Club to the buildings fronting the marina and cordoned off with police tape, Betts pulled over. A uniformed police officer met them as they climbed out of their car. 'I'm sorry, gentlemen. You'll have to move on.'

Fitzjohn straightened his suit coat before pulling out his warrant card. 'I'm DCI Fitzjohn, Constable. This is DS Betts. We're from Day Street Police Station. We've been called in regarding this investigation.'

'I beg your pardon, sir.' The constable lifted the police tape allowing Fitzjohn and Betts to scurry underneath. 'The victim's in the marina on the pontoon.' Fitzjohn looked along the quarry-tiled walkway between two buildings joined at the far end by a covered balcony on the upper level. 'You'll find DC Reynolds there with the man who found the body, sir.'

'Thanks, Constable.'

Fitzjohn and Betts walked in silence to where the two buildings opened out into the marina, the only sound the lapping of water against the hulls of the yachts moored there. A man, hunched over, his head in his hands, sat at an outside table of the nearby coffee shop. A younger man in a light grey suit stood nearby. He approached Fitzjohn.

'Good morning, sir.'

'Morning,' said Fitzjohn. 'DC Reynolds, is it?'

'Yes.'

'I'm DCI Fitzjohn. This is DS Betts. I dare say you've been expecting us.' Fitzjohn gestured to the man seated at the table.

'That's Nigel Prentice, sir,' offered Reynolds. 'He found the body. I haven't been able to get much out of him other than the fact he was the victim's business partner.'

'He's probably in shock. Stay with him for the time being, Reynolds.' Fitzjohn turned, and followed by Betts, continued along a ramp that led to a pontoon bordered by yachts of varying sizes. A few feet away, a young woman knelt beside the body of a man, his sodden clothes forming a pool of water around him. She looked up and smiled as Fitzjohn approached.

'Chief Inspector Fitzjohn?'

'Yes.'

'I'm Simone Knowles. I'm filling in for Charles Conroy while he's on leave.' Simone got to her feet, towering over Fitzjohn, her lean, wiry frame lending her an air of agility and fitness.

'Pleased to meet you, Simone,' said Fitzjohn. 'This is Detective Sergeant Betts.' Betts tripped as he approached, his eyes riveted on Simone.

'I think we've met, haven't we, Sergeant?' she asked. 'But I can't think where.'

'It was at the running club last Sunday,' said Betts, smiling slightly.

'Ah. So it was.'

'I didn't know you ran, Betts,' said Fitzjohn, looking at his sergeant in surprise.

'I've just taken it up, sir' replied Betts as they each knelt down next to the victim's body.

'As you can see,' said the pathologist, 'the victim received a blow to the left side of the head here.' Simone pointed to the side of the victim's head where blood mixed with the gathering pool of water. 'Resulting, I suspect, in a contre coup.' A puzzled look came across Betts's white face. 'Essentially it means damage to the opposite side of the brain in addition to the initial point of contact. In other words, the brain bouncing around inside the head.' Fitzjohn lifted his gaze to the yacht, where the SOCOs were going about their business in relative silence.

'I take it he received that blow from somewhere on the yacht.'

'Yes,' replied Simone. 'And it happened below deck. Fragments of bone have been found adhering to the side of the sink. Even so, he might still be alive if not for this second injury at the front of his head. It was sustained on deck when his head came into contact with the edge of the instrument panel just forward of the helm. Traces of hair and blood have been found, even though someone's tried to wipe it off.' Simone paused. 'Other than that, he has a couple of torn fingernails, and I can't say for sure at this stage, but I doubt he was alive when he entered the water.'

'In which case he had help,' said Fitzjohn.

'Not an unreasonable assumption. As I said, someone's tried very hard to clean up the blood, both below deck as well as on the instrument panel.'

Fitzjohn looked closer at the victim's fist where a small piece of paper protruded from its grip. 'What's this?'

'Looks like the remains of a page from a book, sir,' said Betts peering closer.

'Mmm. I wonder if that book was the cause of all this.'

'Do you have any idea of the time of death, Simone?' asked Fitzjohn, getting to his feet.

'I'd say somewhere between eight and midnight. I'll be able to be more exact after the post mortem.'

Fitzjohn and Betts left Simone Knowles and made their way back along the ramp to where Reynolds stood. 'Do you know who owns the yacht, Reynolds?' asked Fitzjohn.

'Yes, sir. His name's Graeme Wyngard. He's on his way here now.'

'Good.' Fitzjohn looked over at Nigel Prentice who now sat straighter on his seat, sipping a cup of coffee. 'How's Mr Prentice?'

'Feeling a little better, I think, sir. At least the initial shock seems to have worn off.'

'Good. I'll have a word with him after we've looked in the victim's office.'

Followed by Betts, Fitzjohn made his way up a set of cement steps to the balcony above where he opened a glass door marked Rossi & Prentice Yachting Electronics Pty Ltd. Inside, amidst the activity of the SOCOs, they walked into the office overlooking the marina. Fitzjohn took in the room, its neat appearance giving the impression of exactness at whatever went on normally within its walls. The undisturbed surface of the desk displayed a clean coffee mug, laptop computer and pens and pencils arranged in order of size in the desk organizer. Sat prominently behind the desk on a long narrow cupboard, were two, silver framed, photographs. One of a young woman with shoulder length fair hair and a beaming smile, standing at the helm of a yacht. The other photograph, yellowed with age, showed the victim with what looked like his parents, and perhaps a sister. A briefcase lay open next to the photographs, its contents displaying the same orderliness as the desk and the room.

'It's all very neat and tidy,' remarked Betts.

'It is, Betts. Whoever the killer is, he wasn't interested in anything here.' Fitzjohn gestured to the mobile phone, sitting inside its pocket in the lid of the briefcase. 'Contact Telstra and get a list of all incoming and outgoing calls for that phone, Betts.' As he spoke, Fitzjohn lifted his gaze to the window and the harbour beyond, its waters sparkling in the summer sunshine. 'Let's have a word with Mr Prentice, shall we?'

They emerged on to the balcony outside and descended the steps to find a man of medium build in his mid to late fifties speaking to Reynolds. 'This is Mr Wyngard, Chief Inspector,' said Reynolds as Wyngard pushed passed him.

'I take it this means my sloop will be tied up for the time being. Just how long for, Chief Inspector? I have a race on tomorrow.'

Taken aback by the question and sensing Wyngard's dogged personality, Fitzjohn tried to still his growing irritation before he replied, 'That, I can't say. All I can tell you, at this point, is that you'll be informed when your yacht has been released.' Fitzjohn cleared his throat. 'Tell me, Mr Wyngard, when did you last speak to Michael Rossi?'

'It would have been last Wednesday when I booked my yacht in for the alterations. I rang him again on Friday before I brought it in, but Nigel, over there, said Mike was out of town for the weekend.'

'Why did you want to speak to Michael Rossi on Friday?'

'Because I wanted to make sure my yacht would be ready to pick up on Sunday morning. As I said before, I have a race on.' Wyngard's eyes narrowed. 'Will there be anything else, Chief Inspector?'

'No. We'll be in touch, Mr Wyngard.'

As the disgruntled Wyngard left, Fitzjohn turned to Nigel Prentice who still sat in silence sipping his coffee, his face drawn and pale.

'I'm Detective Chief Inspector Fitzjohn, Mr Prentice.' Fitzjohn sat down on a chair opposite. 'Do you feel up to answering a few questions?'

Nigel Prentice nodded, dabbing his forehead with the handkerchief in his shaking hand. 'It's hard to believe this has happened,' he said, looking out across the marina. 'Who would want to do this to Mike?' Fitzjohn, sensing Prentice's distress, waited before he continued.

'I understand you and Michael Rossi were business partners.'

'We were. Since 2007. Pooled our resources to get the business up and running.' Prentice gave a nervous laugh.

'Can you tell me what time you arrived here this morning?'

'It was fairly early,' answered Prentice, putting his handkerchief into his pocket. 'Around seven o'clock. Reason being, I still had work to do on Graeme Wyngard's yacht. He wanted to pick it up first thing on Sunday morning, you see.'

'Did you notice anything different when you arrived? From the usual, that is.'

'Yes, I did. The door to the office was unlocked and Mike's desk lamp was on. Not unusual in itself, but he had told me he'd be away all weekend. I figured he must have changed his plans and was down in the marina working on Wyngard's yacht, so I went down. That's when I found him... in the water underneath the pontoon.' Prentice winced. 'His leg was caught between the pontoon and the yacht. Poor bastard... Mike didn't deserve tha...' Prentice took his handkerchief out of his pocket again and blew his nose.

Fitzjohn waited before he asked, 'Can you tell me when you last spoke to Mr Rossi?'

'Yes. It was early on Friday morning. He called into the office before he drove up to the Hunter Valley. He said he had an appointment with a real estate agent there.'

'Did he plan on buying a property?'

'Selling one, actually. Five Oaks Winery. It's been in his family for many years. It's where he grew up.'

'I see. And did you have any further contact with Mr Rossi after he left for the winery?'

'No, although, I did try to call him on his mobile, but it was turned off so I left a message.'

'What was the message?'

'It was just to tell him who'd telephoned the office that morning. He liked to be kept informed, even when he was away.'

'Who were these people, Mr Prentice?'

'Oh. Let's see. There were three. Graeme Wyngard, calling about his yacht. Another was Rob Nesbit, and...' Nigel Prentice rubbed his forehead and sighed.

'Take your time, Mr Prentice,' said Fitzjohn.

'I'm sorry, Chief Inspector. This is ridiculous. I can't seem to think straight. Oh, that's right. It was Percy Green.'

'All clients are they?'

'Only Wyngard. The other two are... were acquaintances of Mike's.' Prentice paused. 'I can't understand it. Mike was very definite that he wouldn't be back in the office until Monday morning. Something must have gone wrong for him to change his mind.'

'Why do you say that?' asked Fitzjohn.

'Because Mike was a fastidious man. Always had everything worked out. Rarely did he deviate from his plans.'

Fitzjohn's thoughts went to the victim's office and the image its extreme neatness projected. 'Did he appear troubled when he left here on Friday morning?'

'No, not at all. In fact, I haven't seen him quite so relaxed for a long time. He was looking forward to getting the winery listed for sale. Couldn't talk about anything else.' A thoughtful look crossed Nigel Prentice's face. 'I think he saw it as a means of moving on with his life. You see, Chief Inspector, before her death, his sister, Claudia Rossi, had seen to the winery's management. I believe the place reminded him of her.'

'When did she die, Mr Prentice?'

'Oh, it must be almost two years ago now.'

'Did she live at the winery?'

'No. She lived here in Sydney with her partner, Richard Edwards. She employed a winemaker to manage the winery, although she did spend a lot of time there.'

The family photograph of the Rossi family on the cabinet in the victim's office came into Fitzjohn's mind. 'The photographs on the bureau in Michael Rossi's office, Mr Prentice...'

'Yes,' said Prentice, jumping in. The large one is of Mike with his parents and Claudia. The other photograph is of Charlotte Rossi, Claudia's daughter.'

'So Claudia Rossi never married.'

'She did marry when she was young. To John Merrell. He was a yachtsman. You might have heard of him. He was quite well known. He died at sea not long after Charlotte was born. Apparently, after his death, Claudia reverted to her maiden name.' Prentice looked out to the pontoon where Michael Rossi's body laid. 'I still can't believe this has happened.'

'Does anyone other than yourself and Mr Rossi have access to your offices?' continued Fitzjohn.

'Yes. Charlotte has a key. She comes in occasionally to help out, and... I'm not sure, but Stella might also have a key.'

'Stella?'

'Stella Rossi, Mike's wife. Although, they were separated. She used to work in the business before the breakup.'

'On friendly terms were they?'

'I suppose as friendly as you can be after a separation.'

'Do you know if Stella Rossi had been in touch with Michael Rossi lately?'

'I have no idea, Chief Inspector. Mike wasn't the type to share his personal life.'

'I see. Are you aware of any problems he might have had involving other people?'

Nigel Prentice sat in thought for a moment. 'Not really, although, there was that trouble with his winemaker.'

'The same one his sister had hired before her death?'

'Yes. I think his name's Whitehead. As a matter of fact, he called in to see Mike on Thursday.' Prentice's eyebrows rose. 'They argued.'

'Do you know what they argued about?'

'No, I went outside until Mr Whitehead had left,' answered Prentice.

'Do you know where Mr Whitehead can be contacted?'

'No, but I'm sure Charlotte will know.'

'Very well, Mr Prentice, there's just one more thing. Can I ask where you were on Friday evening between the hours of eight and midnight?' With a look of bewilderment, Nigel Prentice hesitated as if trying to remember. 'Take your time, Mr Prentice.'

'It's all right. I was at a council meeting in Woollahra.'

'Are you a member of that council?'

'No, I went there to address council about the parking on my street.' Prentice shook his head. 'Seems so trivial now.'

'Did you go alone to the meeting?'

'Yes. My wife had other plans.'

'Was anyone at the meeting who can verify your attendance? A neighbour perhaps.'

'No, but I did complete a Public Forum Registration form before the meeting started, so my attendance is on record.'

'What time did you leave the meeting, Mr Prentice?'

'When it finished. Shortly before ten, I think it was.'

'And where did you go from there?'

'I went straight home.'

'So you would have arrived home at what time?'

'About ten o'clock. I live close by.'

'Very well, Mr Prentice,' said Fitzjohn, getting to his feet. 'I think we'll leave it there for now, although, I dare say we'll need to speak to you again at some stage.' Fitzjohn paused. 'Oh. There's just one more thing. Charlotte Rossi…'

'Oh, God. She'll have to be told,' said Prentice.

'We'll see to that, sir, if you'll be kind enough to give Detective Sergeant Betts her contact details.'

'Yes. Yes, of course. I'll do that.'

Fitzjohn studied Prentice's vague expression. 'Will you be all right to get yourself home?' he asked. 'Otherwise, I can have one of my officers take you.'

Prentice shook his head. 'That won't be necessary. I'll be fine if I can just sit here for a bit longer.'

In the morning's building humidity, Fitzjohn and Betts left Reynolds in charge of the crime scene and walked back out on to New Beach Road. There, they were met by a barrage of media. 'Can you give us a statement?' shouted one reporter, thrusting his microphone at Fitzjohn's face. Betts stood to one side as Fitzjohn lifted the police tape, and joined the mob.

'All I can say at this stage is that the body of a local businessman was found early this morning in the waters of the marina here at Rushcutters Bay. We're treating the matter as suspicious, therefore I'd ask anyone who was in the vicinity of New Beach Road last evening, and believes they have information, to please come forward.'

'Can you give any more details about what happened?' asked another reporter.'

'I'm afraid it's too early in our investigation. We'll be holding a press conference a little later.' Fitzjohn turned away and followed Betts to the car.

'With any luck, that'll help jog the memory of anyone who did see anything unusual here last night,' he said, taking a handkerchief from his pocket and mopping his brow. Inside the car, he sat back in the passenger seat, savouring the cooling effects of the air conditioning system.

'I didn't know you were a runner, Betts.'

'I'm not, sir.' Betts pulled away from the curb. 'Or at least I wasn't until Chief Superintendent Grieg decided Day Street Police Station would enter a team into the Sydney to Surf Fun Run this year.'

'And you volunteered for that punishment?' asked Fitzjohn, his face aghast.

'It was that or find myself moved to some country town according to the Chief. Actually, the running hasn't been that bad since I joined the running club. I've been pleasantly surprised.' A slight smile crossed Betts's face.

'What with, the running or one of its female members?'

'I suppose, if I'm being honest, it's the latter. I don't think I'm really cut out for running, sir.' Betts paused. 'But I'll suffer through.'

Betts turned the car around. 'Nigel Prentice said we'd find Charlotte Rossi at the victim's house this morning, sir. It's not far. Just back along New Beach Road, opposite Rushcutters Bay Park.'

The black wrought iron gate opened into a small mani-
cured garden where a low, light green, hedge bordered
a tiled path that led to the front door. While Betts rang
the bell, Fitzjohn looked out across Rushcutters Bay Park, brac-
ing himself for his most loathed task, telling a loved one that
their family member would not be coming home. As the front
door opened, Fitzjohn turned back to see a slender young woman
wearing a yellow polo shirt and jeans, the same young woman
who had appeared in the photograph in the victim's office.

'Can I help you?' she asked with a breezy air, and displaying the
same infectious smile.

'We'd like to speak to Charlotte Rossi,' said Fitzjohn.

'I'm Charlotte.'

'We're from the New South Wales Police, Ms Rossi. I'm
Detective Chief Inspector Fitzjohn, and this is Detective Sergeant
Betts.' Both Fitzjohn and Betts held up their warrant cards. 'Nigel
Prentice said we might find you here.'

'Nigel? Is something wrong?'

'I'm afraid so. May we come in?'

The smile disappeared from Charlotte Rossi's face as she stepped back from the doorway. 'Come through.' They followed her along the hall, up a short flight of stairs and into a large rectangular living area overlooking Rushcutters Bay. Another woman in her late forties with brown wavy hair and a curvaceous shape, stood with her back to them looking at a large sketch hung on the wall at the far end of the room. Dressed in white slacks and black top, she turned when they appeared.

'This is my friend, Phillipa Braithwaite,' said Charlotte Rossi. 'These gentlemen are from the police, Phil.' Charlotte gestured for Fitzjohn and Betts to sit down before settling herself on the edge of an armchair, a questioning look on her oval shaped face. Phillipa Braithwaite seated herself on the arm of a small sofa, adjusting the gold bracelets on her wrists before crossing her long legs. 'Why are you here?' asked Charlotte, a tinge of uncertainty in her voice.

'It's your uncle, Ms Rossi. Michael Rossi's body was found early this morning...'

'His body?' Charlotte Rossi's voice rang out, a look of disbelief coming to her face. 'You mean Michael is dead?'

'I'm afraid so.'

'But that can't be.' Charlotte paused, glaring at Fitzjohn before she continued in a whisper. 'What happened to him?'

'All I can tell you at this stage is that we're treating your uncle's death as suspicious. As I was about to say, his body was found this morning at the marina outside his business premises.

'But he's supposed to be in the Hunter Valley this weekend. I don't understand.'

'In that case, if you can tell us when you last saw your uncle, Ms Rossi, it might help us to find out why he was here in Sydney.'

Charlotte Rossi swallowed hard. 'I saw him yesterday morning around seven. He called at my flat to drop off the keys to his house because he planned to be away all weekend, and he needed someone to be here when his new fridge arrives. That's what Phillipa and me are doing here. Waiting... for the fridge.' Charlotte Rossi fell silent before she continued. 'He won't need it now, will he?' She grabbed a tissue from the box on the coffee table.

'Do you feel able to answer a few questions, Ms Rossi, or would you prefer we come back later?'

'No, I'll be right.' She ran her index finger along the bottom eyelashes of her right eye, stemming a tear. 'What do you want to know?' she sniffed.

'We understand your uncle owned a winery in the Hunter Valley.'

'Yes. That's right. Five Oaks Winery. It's been in our family since... since my grandparents moved to the Hunter in the early 1950s. They're both gone now.' Charlotte's brow furrowed. 'Michael had arranged to meet a real estate agent there so he could have the property listed for sale. He said he'd be driving back early on Monday morning.' Charlotte pulled another tissue from the box and dabbed her nose.

'Was that the last time you spoke to him?' asked Fitzjohn.

'Yes. It was.'

'Is there anyone at the winery we can speak to? If so, there's every chance we'll be able to find out why your uncle returned to Sydney early.'

'There's Rafe Simms. He has the property next door. He's been helping out for the past few weeks since the…' Fitzjohn waited for Charlotte Rossi to continue. 'Oh, it's not important.'

'In this situation, Ms Rossi, everything's important.'

'I suppose it is. I didn't think. I was just about to say that Rafe has been managing the winery since our winemaker, Pierce Whitehead, left.'

'Why did Mr Whitehead leave?'

'I don't know. Michael didn't offer any explanation. He just told me Pierce quit.' Charlotte Rossi sighed. 'I didn't press him for details.' Charlotte met Fitzjohn's intense gaze. 'It would have just annoyed Michael and, at the time, I didn't feel like a confrontation with him. Besides, I think I know why Pierce quit. He and Michael often clashed when Michael visited the winery. Pierce didn't like Michael's interference.' Charlotte Rossi paused. 'You see, Chief Inspector, Pierce was hired by my mother in 2010. He had a five-year contract. It wasn't until after her death that Michael had to have anything to do with the winery, or Pierce. I suppose, in the end, it just got the better of Pierce. He walked off the property two weeks ago, right in the middle of the grape harvest.' Charlotte threw her hands in the air. 'The whole thing culminated in Michael deciding to sell the winery. That's when Rafe Simms stepped in. He offered to finish the harvest and buy the grapes.'

'Do you know where Mr Whitehead can be contacted?' asked Fitzjohn.

'I'm sorry, I don't. But his phone number will be in my phone because he rang me last night.'

'Oh? What was the reason for his call?'

'He wanted to know if I'd be a referee for a job he's applying for in a Victorian winery.'

'And did you agree?'

'Yes. I couldn't see any reason not to. He was an excellent wine-maker. He'd proved that over the last couple of years. I think his sudden departure from Five Oaks Winery was more to do with his inability to get on with my uncle than anything else. And as far as his present whereabouts, I'm sure his details will be in the study. Michael would have kept them for superannuation and tax purposes. I'll have a look for you.' Charlotte Rossi rose from her chair. As she did so, she steadied herself on its arm. 'The study is this way, Chief Inspector.' Fitzjohn and Betts followed Charlotte out of the living room, and into a room overlooking a small courtyard. 'She crossed to the bookcase and reached for a folder. 'That's odd.'

'What is it?' asked Fitzjohn.

'It's my uncle's overnight bag. He must have left it in here when he got back from the winery.' She pointed to a bag on the floor beside the desk, its zipper half-undone. 'I don't understand. Michael would not normally leave his bag here.' She looked at Fitzjohn. 'He was organised to the extreme. Nothing ever out of place. Compulsive, obsessive, I think you'd call it.'

Betts knelt down to look inside the bag. 'It doesn't look like it's been unpacked, sir.'

'Right,' said Fitzjohn. 'Have forensics come in to look over the room and the rest of the house, Betts.' Fitzjohn then turned back to Charlotte Rossi, her eyes fixed on the bag. Sensing her anguish he said, 'Is this the folder, Ms Rossi?'

Charlotte shot a look at Fitzjohn. 'Yes.'

Fitzjohn took the folder and ushered her back toward the living room. As he did so, he took in the sleek lines of the white con-temporary sofas, chairs and glass topped tables that imparted a feeling of austerity. Charlotte sat down. 'There's just one more question I have to ask, Ms Rossi,' said Fitzjohn. 'Can you tell us where you were between the hours of eight and midnight last evening?' Phillipa Braithwaite gave Fitzjohn a disparaging look.

'Yes. I closed the shop at around 6pm,' replied Charlotte. 'It's a bookshop. In Double Bay. After closing up, I stayed on to do some paperwork until about nine.'

'And what time did you receive the telephone call from Pierce Whitehead?'

Charlotte Rossi removed her mobile phone from her handbag and after pressing some buttons, handed it to Fitzjohn. 'As you can see, it was twenty-six minutes past seven.'

'Did you see or speak to anyone else yesterday evening?'

'No,' she said as Fitzjohn handed the phone back.

'Very well, Ms Rossi.' Fitzjohn got to his feet. 'We'll leave it at that for now. I'm sorry we've had to bring you this news. Please accept our condolences.'

Fitzjohn and Betts emerged from the house and made their way back along the garden pathway to their car. 'I couldn't live in that place,' said Betts. 'It's so… uncluttered.'

'It's called minimalism, Betts. If you remember, Michael Rossi's office was the same. I'd say he was an orderly, exacting man and, no doubt, expected the same of those around him.'

'Sounds to me like he was just plain difficult to get on with,' replied Betts.

{CHAPTER 5}

Fitzjohn and Betts arrived at Kings Cross Police Station fifteen minutes later, and made their way into the building. 'Alistair, I heard you were being seconded.' Fitzjohn looked around to see an old colleague, himself a Detective Chief Inspector. 'It's been a while,' said Ron Carling.

'It has.' Fitzjohn smiled, acknowledging the tall, heavy-set man, and remembering their days together as rookie constables.

'I've not seen you out on the course lately. Given up golf have you?'

'I've been captured by my late wife's orchids.' Fitzjohn caught Ron Carling's questioning look before turning to Betts who lingered behind. 'This is my Sergeant, Martin Betts.' Carling nodded toward Betts.

'It's good to have you both on board. You've probably been told we're strapped at the moment. Come through.' Ron Carling opened the inner door to the station, and followed by Betts, he and Fitzjohn made their way along the corridor.

'I'm surprised Grieg agreed to your secondment, Alistair. How does he know he'll get you back?' asked Ron.

'If I know Grieg, he's hoping he doesn't.' Fitzjohn chuckled to himself.

'I take it your working relationship hasn't improved.'

'Not in the least. And since Grieg's been bumped up to Chief Superintendent, it can only get worse.'

'Yes, I heard about his promotion.' Carling grimaced. 'Then all I can say is enjoy the respite.'

Carling stopped and opened a door to his right. 'I've managed to secure this Incident Room for you, and an investigative team.' The door opened into a large room full of desks and a white board at the far end. 'As it turns out, it's also your office, I'm afraid. Sorry about that, Alistair. We're short of space.'

Fitzjohn looked around, his thoughts going to his small, but familiar office at Day Street Police Station that provided a degree of solitude and comfort. 'This'll be just fine, Ron, and thanks.'

As Ron Carling left, Fitzjohn turned to Betts. 'Well, for the foreseeable future, it looks like this is home. Let's get settled.' Fitzjohn made his way to the far end of the room, placing his briefcase on the desk beside the whiteboard. He took off his suit coat, hung it on the back of the chair and rubbed his hands together. 'We'll start by going through what we have so far, Betts.'

———◦◦◦———

Later that same morning, the investigative team gathered for their meeting, the banter in the room dwindling as Fitzjohn got to his feet. 'Good morning all,' he said, pushing his glasses up along the bridge of his nose. 'For those who don't know me,

I'm DCI Fitzjohn from Day Street Police Station. I've been seconded, along with DS Betts, here, to head this investigation. I'm hoping that with your help and expertise it will be solved quickly.' Fitzjohn turned to the whiteboard.

'By now, I'm sure you'll all have familiarized yourselves with the details of the case. The victim, Michael Rossi, aged forty-nine, was found early this morning by his business partner, Nigel Prentice, at the marina in front of their place of business at Rushcutters Bay.' A slight rumbling went through the room from those gathered. 'The exact time of death and the cause, has yet to be determined.'

An hour later, Fitzjohn sat back in his chair as those in attendance, save Betts and Reynolds, gradually dispersed to their individual pursuits. As they did so, Fitzjohn smiled, looking to one remaining officer. 'Detective Constable Williams, I thought that was you in the crowd.'

Williams beamed. 'It's Detective Senior Constable now, sir.'

'Congratulations,' replied Fitzjohn. 'Don't tell me you've also been seconded.'

'No. While you were away on leave, I was permanently moved, at Chief Superintendent Grieg's request.'

'Ah. Any explanation why?'

'No, but it's okay. I'm happy with the change.'

Fitzjohn thought back to the last time Williams had worked with him on his investigative team at Day Street Station. He remembered him as a sallow looking young man with a sullen disposition and dry sense of humour. The dry wit was still evident, but Williams looked transformed. He actually looked happy. 'Well, Williams, the change appears to have done wonders for you. Perhaps you'd like to work with Reynolds, here, in checking out Nigel Prentice's alibi,' Fitzjohn looked to Reynolds, 'and then I'd like you both to speak to Rafe Simms at the winery. I want to know if he has any idea why the victim returned to Sydney earlier than planned.'

As Williams and Reynolds left, Fitzjohn sat back in his chair, took his glasses off and rubbed his face before he said, 'Well Betts, what do we have. A victim with an uncompromising personality. So one could assume he provoked those he came into contact with. His winemaker, Pierce Whitehead, being one of them.'

'Even so, quitting as winemaker couldn't have been in his best interest,' offered Betts. 'Maybe that's why Whitehead went to see the victim on Thursday. To ask for his job back.'

'And possibly got turned down, resulting in their argument,' replied Fitzjohn. 'Michael Rossi doesn't sound, to me, like the forgiving type. And that's why we'll start by speaking to Pierce Whitehead.'

The Duty Officer appeared at the door as Fitzjohn got to his feet. 'There's someone here to see you, Chief Inspector. A Mrs Timmons. She wouldn't say what it's about.'

'Can you take care of it, Sergeant? We're just about to leave,' said Fitzjohn, pulling on his suit coat.

'I tried that, sir, but she's very determined. She insists on speaking to you.'

Fitzjohn sighed. 'Oh, very well.'

❖{CHAPTER 6}❖

Esme Timmons placed her steaming cup of tea on the small table next to her armchair and sat down heavily. Her escapade in the early hours of the morning had left her with a badly bruised hip and elbow. Still, she did not regret challenging last night's intruder. In fact, the thought sent a rush of exhilaration through her. Had her cane made contact? She looked over to where it now lay on the dining room table, its silver handle glinting in the morning sun. She should, she supposed, mention it to Michael. But perhaps not. He would make such a fuss.

It was then that the morning news bulletin took Esme's attention. With her cup poised at her lips, she put it down and listened to the crisp English voice of a plain clothed police officer reporting the death of a local businessman at Rushcutters Bay, and asking anyone who had been in the vicinity of New Beach Road the previous evening, to come forward. New Beach Road, thought Esme. I know New Beach Road. Isn't that where... At that moment, the screen switched back to the newsreader and Michael's name rang out. Esme's eyes glistened with tears.

Unaware of the time, she sat transfixed to the television screen long after the broadcast ended, a feeling of sadness sweeping over her. Eventually she rose from her chair, and made her way into the kitchen placing her cup in the sink, her mind trying to grasp what she had heard. They were both gone now. Michael and Claudia. Through a haze of tears, Esme looked out of the window and into the garden. A lush, green retreat on a warm summer's day. Claudia had loved the garden. Esme struggled to push away a growing despondence, her thoughts going back to last evening. Did Michael's unexpected appearance have anything to do with his death? And what about that intruder? They had both been in Claudia's study, after all. Was it merely coincidence?

———— ⋙◆⋘ ————

An hour later, dressed in a light blue cotton dress, Esme stood in front of the hall mirror running a comb through her silver grey hair before placing a wide brimmed straw hat on her head. Adding a little lipstick to her lips, she picked up her handbag and walking cane, with its silver handle now captured inside a plastic bag, and left the house.

Ten minutes later, Esme arrived at Waverton train station, and made her way to the ticket counter. 'A return pensioner's concession to Kings Cross, please,' she said to the unsmiling Indian man on the other side of the window.

'You'll have to change at Town Hall, madam,' he replied.

Esme nodded and gathered up her ticket and change before taking the elevator down to the platform. There, she settled herself on a blue painted bench and waited. As she did so, a welcomed gust of air rushed past her, dissipating the heat for a few seconds before the train arrived. Gathering her handbag and cane, she climbed aboard, sitting in the first seat by the door. The only other occupant of that space was a youth with earphones plugged into each ear, his eyes riveted to the floor. Thinking what damage he must be doing to his hearing, Esme sighed and looked ahead at the advertisement displayed on the wall in front of her. A photograph of The Three Sisters rock formation in the Blue Mountains. It brought back a long forgotten memory of reading the Aboriginal dreamtime legend of The Three Sisters to her young students. A hint of a smile came to Esme's face. Half an hour later, after changing at Town Hall, the train arrived at Kings Cross Station and Esme made her way out of the station, and back into the stifling heat.

Although she had never been to Kings Cross, Esme knew of its sordid reputation so she took great interest in each establishment as she made her way up along Darlinghurst Road. For the most part, it was deserted except for a few people sitting at outdoor cafés reading their morning papers, and sipping their coffee. Of course, early on a Saturday morning was probably not the time to see the place in full swing, thought Esme. Presently, she came to Fitzroy Gardens, a green oasis amid the hubbub of the city where she paused to catch her breath at the El Alamein Memorial Fountain. Made up of dozens of small spray heads that formed a round sphere, it resembled a large thistle, the resulting fine spray moving gently into the breeze providing a cooling effect. Esme lingered a moment to read the plaque commemorating those who had fallen in battle before carrying on to the Kings Cross Police Station on the other side of the Gardens. Feeling a twinge in her hip, she chose to walk along the wheelchair ramp to the front door. Once inside the cool air-conditioned building, she approached the glass fronted counter.

'Good morning, madam, can I help you,' came a voice from behind the glass.

'Yes. My name is Esme Timmons, and I'm here to speak to Detective Chief Inspector Fitzjohn. I believe he's from this station.'

'He is, madam, but I'm afraid he's unavailable at the moment. Can I help you, perhaps?'

'No, I need to speak to the Chief Inspector personally. How long do you think he'll be?'

'It could be up to an hour, madam.'

'Oh. That's a pity.' Esme sighed. 'Very well. I'll just have to wait. At least it's cool in here. The train that brought me from the city didn't have any air con.' With a quick smile, Esme glanced around and spied the chairs lining the lobby. 'I'll wait over there.'

Twenty minutes passed before a man in his mid-fifties appeared. Of medium height and impeccably dressed in a dark blue suit, crisp white shirt with a light blue tie, he adjusted his wire-framed glasses as he approached. Esme knew, at once, that this was the Detective Chief Inspector she had seen on the television news that morning.

'Good morning, madam. I'm Detective Chief Inspector Fitzjohn. I understand you wish to speak to me.'

Remembering the pleasant tone of his voice and his English accent, Esme got to her feet and extended her hand. 'Yes, I do, Chief Inspector. My name's Esme Timmons and I've come to see you about my nephew, Michael Rossi. I learnt of his death this morning on the news.'

The Detective Chief Inspector appeared to hesitated before he said, 'My apologies for keeping you waiting, Mrs Timmons, I wasn't aware of the reason you wanted to see me. I'm very sorry for your loss, and the manner in which you received the news. It's regrettable.'

'Well, whatever way one receives such news, it's a shock to the system. Even so, I felt the need to speak to you.'

'I'm afraid there's little I can tell you at this stage.'

'Oh, I realise that,' replied Esme. 'I came because I believe you'll be piecing together my nephew's movements over the past twenty-four hours, and I wanted to tell you that he came to see me last evening.'

'I see. Well, in that case, would you mind coming through to my office?'

'No, not at all.' Esme picked up her handbag and the walking cane. 'And it's *Miss* Timmons.'

'Oh. I beg your pardon.'

'That's all right. It happens a lot,' said Esme, as they walked together along the corridor and into a large room.

Esme hesitated in the doorway as she looked around. 'My, it's a big office you have, isn't it? Reminds me of a school room.' A quick smile came to Esme's face. 'I worked as a teacher in my younger days.'

At the far side of the room, a ginger-haired young man scrambled to his feet.

'This is Detective Sergeant Betts, Miss Timmons. Miss Timmons is Michael Rossi's aunt, Betts.'

Fitzjohn pulled out the chair in front of his desk. 'Please, have a seat, Miss Timmons. Would you care for a cool drink or a cup of tea, perhaps?'

'A cup of tea would be most welcome, Chief Inspector. I'm quite parched after my journey.'

Fitzjohn glanced at Betts, smiling as he did so. 'I wouldn't mind a cup myself, Betts.'

While Betts left the room, Esme, grasping her cane with its plastic covered handle, settled herself into the chair.

'You said your nephew came to see you last night, Miss Timmons.'

'Yes. Michael calls in from time to time to see how I am. Of course now... well...' She paused, trying to prevent her growing despondency taking hold. 'Anyway, last night, he arrived a few minutes after six. I know because I'd just sat down to watch the SBS World News. It was unusual. That he called at that time, I mean. You see, he knows I have dinner then, and that I like to watch the news. It alerted me to the fact there might be something wrong.'

'And was there?'

'He never said, although I sensed his distress. All he seemed interested in was looking through Claudia's study for some letters.' Esme noticed the Chief Inspectors questioning look. 'Claudia was Michael's twin sister. She died just over a year ago, poor dear.'

'I take it your niece lived with you before she died, Miss Timmons.'

'No, she didn't. She just used one of the upstairs rooms in my house as a study, and for her restoration work. She freelanced as an art restorer, you see, besides working at the New South Wales Art Gallery. The room is as she left it, filled with her books and paraphernalia.' Esme sighed. 'I didn't have the heart to throw any of it away.'

'And your nephew said he was looking for some letters?'

'Yes. I don't know that he found them though. He didn't say.'
Esme paused. 'I wouldn't blame you for thinking this is all irrel-
evant to your investigation, Chief Inspector, and I wouldn't have
thought much about it myself, but for the intruder.'

'Intruder?' Fitzjohn sat straighter in his chair.

'Oh, didn't I mention that?' Esme smiled. 'That's what's irri-
tating about being older. One tends to forget things from time to
time. Well, the fact is, I first heard the upstairs floorboards creak
at twenty-three minutes past two this morning. It gave me quite
a start, I can tell you.' Esme eyed Fitzjohn speculatively. 'I expect
you're thinking I imagined the whole thing, but you'd be wrong
because I went upstairs to have a look, and I saw the intruder
coming out of Claudia's study. That's when I walloped him with
my cane. And in case you're wondering, that's why my cane has
a plastic bag over the handle. I thought there might be forensic
evidence on it.' A stunned Fitzjohn continued his silence as Esme
handed him the cane. 'I must have fainted after that because the
next thing I remember, I was lying on the floor.'

'Are you injured in any way, Miss Timmons?' asked Fitzjohn,
showing concern.

'It's hard to tell. At my age, one tends to have aches and creaking sensations on a daily basis, but other than a bruised hip, I
think I'm fine.'

Fitzjohn and Esme both looked around as the door opened
and Betts backed into the room carrying a tray. 'I thought I'd join
you,' he said, placing the tray on Fitzjohn's desk before pulling up
a chair. 'Milk, Miss Timmons?'

Fitzjohn drummed his fingers on the desk.

'Yes. Thank you, Sergeant. You're very kind. I hope all this is of
some help, Chief Inspector,' said Esme, looking back at Fitzjohn.

'I know it's vital at the start of an investigation to get as much information as possible. At least that's what I'm led to believe. I read a lot of crime fiction, and of course, there's the nightly news.'

'I can assure you, Miss Timmons, your efforts are much appreciated. As you've just said, it's important to gather as much information as possible, as soon as possible.' Fitzjohn sipped his tea. 'What would really help is if you can tell us what time your nephew left your house last night.'

'It was just after seven.'

'Did he take anything with him?'

'He did have a book under his arm when he left. It had a black leather cover. You never know, if he had found the letters, he might have popped them inside.' Esme hesitated. 'I'm sorry to be so vague, Chief Inspector. At the time, I wasn't taking much notice.'

'Did he say where he was going?'

'Mmm. There again, I didn't take a lot of notice. I wanted to get back to my dinner. But I seem to remember him saying he was going to call around and see Charlotte. She's Claudia's daughter, and my great-niece.'

'Charlotte Rossi?'

'Yes.' Esme frowned. 'Have you spoken to her?'

'We have. Early this morning.'

'Oh, the poor dear. I did try to ring her before I left the house this morning, but there was no answer.'

'We found her at your nephew's house, Miss Timmons. Apparently, waiting to accept the delivery of a fridge.'

'I see.'

'She wasn't alone. A woman by the name of Phillipa Braithwaite was with her.'

'Oh, thank goodness for that. It makes me feel a bit better. It's terrible to receive such news when you're alone. More so, I think, when you're young like Charlotte. Phillipa Braithwaite was Claudia's friend. From school days. They lost touch, but were reunited a few years ago. After Claudia died, Phillipa took Charlotte under her wing, so to speak.'

'I see. Where do you live, Miss Timmons?' asked Fitzjohn.

'Waverton. I've lived there all my life. I stayed on in my parents' house when my fiancé failed to return from the Korean War.' Esme paused for a moment in reflection. 'It was 1953. He was very young. Twenty-three. Seems like yesterday.' Esme gave a slight smile.

'It's been quite a journey for you all the way from the North Shore, Miss Timmons. Detective Sergeant Betts and I will be happy to escort you home.'

'Well, that's very kind. And I think I might accept. I was a bit worried about getting home again. The later in the day it gets, the busier the trains will be. It'll also give you the opportunity to have a look through Claudia's study. You never know, it could aid your investigation.'

Fitzjohn smiled. 'A good suggestion, Miss Timmons.'

Esme's home, nestled amongst the trees and shrubs in her garden, exuded elegant charm of a bygone era. Fitzjohn pushed the wrought iron gate open and let Esme pass though. 'Well, this is home, Chief Inspector,' she said, taking her keys out of her handbag and leading the way along the garden path to the house. 'Unfortunately, you're not seeing the garden at its best. It misses

Claudia's tender touch, I'm afraid.' They ascended the steps to the front verandah where two white whicker armchairs, yellowed by age, gave further evidence of an era long past. Esme unlocked the front door and stepped inside. 'Come in, gentlemen,' she said, putting her handbag on the hall table. 'You'll find Claudia's study upstairs at the end of the hall.' Esme removed her straw hat. 'I'm sure you'll forgive me if I don't accompany you. I don't think my legs will take those stairs again today. And, at the moment, I don't think I can face seeing the mess the study's been left in.' As the two police officers disappeared upstairs, Esme looked into the mirror above the hall table. 'Oh, you look a fright,' she muttered. She replaced her lipstick, studied herself in the mirror again, and made her way to the kitchen, to the sound of floorboards creaking above. Unlike the previous evening, the sound gave her a renewed sense of security. Making the most of that feeling, Esme made tea, later wheeling the tea trolley, complete with chocolate cake, into the living room, where she sat down and waited.

Sometime later, the Chief Inspector and his Sergeant reappeared. 'I've made some refreshment for you both,' she said. 'I'll let you pour your own.'

'That's very kind, Miss Timmons. Thank you.' Fitzjohn poured himself a cup of tea, while Betts eyed the chocolate cake. 'Did you notice anything missing from the study, Miss Timmons?' he asked, settling himself into an armchair.

'It's hard to tell with the books and papers strewn everywhere. Hannah may know.' Esme noted Fitzjohn's questioning look. 'She comes in to clean on Friday mornings. Yesterday she vacuumed and dusted upstairs.'

'Then we must speak to her,' said Fitzjohn, sipping his tea. 'I'd also like to call in our forensic team. I'm sure they won't inconvenience you too much, and it might help us to ascertain whether there's a connection between last night's break-in and your nephew's death.'

'If there is a connection,' said Esme, 'I suppose there's every possibility the intruder might return.'

'Is there anyone you can stay with, Miss Timmons? For the time being.'

'So you do think there's a possibility of the intruder returning,' said Esme, with a glint in her eye. 'But to answer your question, Chief Inspector. I daresay I could go and stay with Charlotte, but I prefer to stay here.'

Moments later, Esme saw Fitzjohn and Betts to the front door where she said goodbye before returning to her armchair in the living room. A void had been created by their short stay and Esme felt it sweeping over her now, bringing with it a feeling of loneliness. She had felt it before, of course, after Tom failed to return from Korea in 1953, and then again, when both her parents had passed away, and she found herself alone. But this time it was different. Michael's life had been taken from him, he did not die because he was fighting for his country, or because he had grown old. Esme sat back and wept.

❮CHAPTER 7❯

Fitzjohn and Betts left Esme Timmons watching the midday news. Outside, Betts opened the wrought iron gate, hanging loosely from its hinges, and followed by Fitzjohn, made his way to the car. 'I can't help but feel sorry for Miss Timmons, sir. Other than her great-niece, Charlotte Rossi, she's now quite alone.'

Fitzjohn listened, somewhat surprised at Betts's empathy. 'She's certainly had her fair share of loss,' he replied. 'Perhaps it would be a good idea for you to be here when the forensics team come in, Betts. Miss Timmons is remarkably stoic, but even so, it might be disconcerting for her to have a bunch of strangers in the house. Especially after the break-in.'

'Do you think the break-in was connected to Michael Rossi's death, sir?' asked Betts, unlocking the car doors.

'It's hard to tell at this stage, but to be on the safe side, I want the Coroner's report into Claudia Rossi's death, and as much information about her as you can lay your hands on.' Fitzjohn settled himself into the passenger seat, removed his glasses, and used the handkerchief from his breast pocket to mop the perspiration from his forehead. 'Where did Miss Timmons say her cleaning lady lives?' he asked.

'In an apartment building on Willoughby Road, sir.'

'Very well, we'll go there first to make arrangements for her to look through the study,' said Fitzjohn, adjusting the flow of cool air on to his face before putting his glasses back on.

Minutes later, they walked into the apartment building, Betts running his eyes down the list of tenants. 'I don't see her name here, sir.'

'Are you sure we have the right address?'

Betts pulled his notebook out and flicked through the pages. 'This is the place all right. Hannah Blair, Unit 17. I suppose she could be living with a flat-mate and not listed.'

'True,' said Fitzjohn, walking back outside.

'Shall I ask Miss Timmons again, sir?'

'No. Stoic she may be, but I don't want to alarm her unnecessarily. Finding out that her cleaning lady might have given a false address is the last thing she needs right now. Besides, I have every confidence you can locate Hannah Blair, Betts. But not until we've been to the morgue. I want to see how Simone Knowles is getting on with our victim.' Fitzjohn sensed Betts's uncharacteristic enthusiasm for what he knew was his Sergeant's least liked task - visiting the morgue. Why doesn't that surprise me, he thought.

An antiseptic odor filled the air as they walked into the Mortuary Office on Arundel Street in Glebe and were told that the post mortem was already in progress. With Betts hanging back, they followed the attendant into a long room dominated by a row of stainless steel tables. Simone Knowles, now clad in her operating theatre garb, stood at one of them. She looked up as they approached.

'Chief Inspector, Sergeant.'

'Sorry we're late,' said Fitzjohn, taking in the scene. 'Have you determined how Mr Rossi died?' he asked.

'Yes. It was from a massive brain haemorrhage, and I was right, the brain injury was a case of contre coup. You might like to take a look.' She smiled at Betts who hovered behind Fitzjohn. 'There are also some fine paper cuts on his right index finger.'

'The hand that the piece of paper was found in?' asked Fitzjohn.

'Yes. Possibly sustained when, whatever he was holding at the time, left his grasp.'

'Have you established the time of death?'

'Between 9:30 and 11.00pm.'

———❊———

They emerged from the morgue to find a slate grey sky and the rumble of thunder in the humid atmosphere. 'Looks like we're in for a storm,' said Fitzjohn looking at the sky before his attention was taken by Betts. 'Are you all right, Betts? You look a bit pale.'

'I'll be fine, sir. It's just the smell of that place. It follows me out of the door.'

'Mmm. I know what you mean. The morgue does have its own particular fragrance. And it does tend to cling.' It was then that Fitzjohn's mobile phone rang.

'Fitzjohn here.' A short silence followed. 'Tell him it's not possible, Sergeant. I'll see what I can do later in the day.' Fitzjohn put his phone back into his pocket.

'It seems Chief Superintendent Grieg wants to see me, Betts, but I think our time is better spent speaking to our victim's winemaker, Pierce Whitehead. Where can we find him?'

'He's been renting an apartment in Annandale, since leaving the winery, sir.'

The downpour came as Fitzjohn and Betts made their way into the twenty-story apartment building on Collins Street. Reaching the lobby, Fitzjohn brushed his suit coat off before pressing the intercom button.

'Hello,' came a sharp, clipped voice.

'Mr Whitehead?'

'Yes, who's this?'

'I'm Detective Chief Inspector Fitzjohn from the New South Wales Police. I have with me Detective Sergeant Betts. We'd like to speak to you, please, sir.' There was no reply only the release of the security door into the building. Fitzjohn and Betts made their way to the elevator and up to the fourteenth floor, amid the muffled sound of thunder. The door to Pierce Whitehead's apartment stood open when they approached, a stocky man of medium height in the doorway.

'I suppose you're here about Mike Rossi.'

'We are, Mr Whitehead,' said Fitzjohn. 'May we come in?' Whitehead stepped back from the doorway before leading the way into the apartment.

'I heard about what happened to Mike on the news this morning,' he said, gesturing to a nestle of armchairs in the living area. 'I thought you'd be along.' After getting seated, Betts returned Whitehead's stare as he took his notebook and pen out of his inside coat pocket.

'Tell me, Mr Whitehead,' said Fitzjohn, 'why did you expect us?'

'Because of my connection to Mike, of course. The very fact you're here tells me that you know of that connection.'

'You're right. We do. We understand you were his winemaker.'

'Until recently, yes.'

'We're also led to believe your departure from that position was, shall we say, somewhat sudden.'

'I don't see what that's got to do with Mike's death.' Whitehead ran his hand through his lengthy brown hair.

'It may not have anything to do with it, Mr Whitehead, but I'm sure you can appreciate that we have to follow every thread of information in an investigation such as this. For instance, I'm curious as to why you left your position as winemaker in the middle of the grape harvest. Surely, as a winemaker, you wanted to see your crop harvested if for no other reason than for your own satisfaction and sense of accomplishment.'

'I didn't have much choice in the matter, Chief Inspector. Mike Rossi fired me.'

'Oh. I see. Why did he do that?'

Whitehead shrugged. 'Who knows? I stopped trying to figure Mike out a long time ago.' Pierce Whitehead met Fitzjohn's intense gaze. 'Okay. We'd disagreed over a few matters concerning the harvest.' He shrugged again. 'Let's face it. I should have left after Claudia died.' Whitehead paused. 'I take it you know about Mike's sister, Claudia.'

'Yes, we understand she was the person who initially employed you as the winemaker at Five Oaks Winery.'

'That's right. And we got on fine. Everything was fine, in fact, until Mike Rossi took over.'

'How well did you know, Claudia Rossi, Mr Whitehead?'

Whitehead looked guarded. 'We had a good working relationship. She was open to advice for producing better wines, and she was interested in wine growing. But other than that, I knew very little about her.'

'Where are you working now?'

'As yet, I haven't found another position. Mike declining to be a referee hasn't made it easy.'

'Is that why you went to see him at his office last Thursday morning?'

'Oh, you know about that too, do you? And, I suppose you also know that we argued.' Fitzjohn did not respond. 'I went to ask Mike whether he would stand as a referee for a position I'm applying for. He refused and I lost my temper.'

'Can I ask where you were between 8pm last night and 4 this morning, Mr Whitehead?'

'I was here. I didn't go out last night.'

'Did you see anyone? Talk to anyone?'

'No. Oh, I take that back. I did talk to Charlotte Rossi. Over the phone.'

'Charlotte Rossi?' Fitzjohn frowned. 'You've kept in touch with her since you left the winery?'

'No. It's just that I'd had no luck with her uncle so I decided to ask Charlotte if she'd be willing to stand as a referee.'

'But wouldn't you need a reference from the owner of the winery?'

'She is an owner. She and Mike Rossi are, or at least were joint owners since Claudia Rossi's death.'

A look of surprise crossed Fitzjohn's face and he thought for a moment before continuing. 'Did Charlotte Rossi agree to be a referee?'

'Yes, she did.'

'And would you say she took an active part in the winery?'

'She didn't when her mother was in charge. I don't think the two of them got on very well. And after Mike took over... well, he wouldn't have welcomed her input.'

———⟫⟨———

Fitzjohn and Betts headed back to Kings Cross Police Station through the rain soaked streets. 'So, Whitehead didn't walk out on the harvest after all,' said Betts. 'He was fired by Michael Rossi. Odd that Charlotte Rossi doesn't appear to be aware of that fact.'

Fitzjohn emerged from his thoughts. 'Perhaps not so odd when you consider what Pierce Whitehead told us. That Charlotte Rossi had never taken an active role in the winery.' Fitzjohn paused. 'I wonder why she and her mother didn't get on. I think we'll speak to her again, Betts. And also, see what you can find out about Pierce Whitehead. There's something about that man, but I just can't put my finger on it.'

———⟫⟨———

Feeling damp from the rain, Fitzjohn removed his suit coat and hung it on the back of his chair before sitting down. Forming a pyramid with his fingers, he eyed Reynolds who sat sprawled in a chair. 'Are we keeping you awake Reynolds,' he asked.

Reynolds shifted suddenly, his notebook falling to the floor. 'Sorry, sir. I didn't get much sleep last night. We have a new baby at home. She cried all night.'

'She's probably lactose intolerant,' offered Williams who stood poised at the whiteboard, 'It causes colic.'

'I didn't realise that you're an expert on babies, Williams,' said Fitzjohn, looking around.

'I have a nephew, sir. He kept my brother-in-law awake for months.'

'And your sister too, no doubt.' Fitzjohn paused. 'Let's get on with what we're here for, shall we? I want to know how you both got on with your inquiries.'

Reynolds scrambled for his notebook and flipped through its pages. 'In relation to Nigel Prentice, sir, I spoke to a member of council who was at last night's meeting. He said Mr Prentice addressed council before leaving the meeting around 8pm.'

'That's interesting.' Fitzjohn watched as Williams added the information to the whiteboard. 'Prentice gave the impression he was at that meeting for its duration. So, where was he between 8 and 10pm?'

'How about you, Williams? Were you able to get on to Rafe Simms?'

'Yes, sir,' answered Williams as he continued writing. 'Mr Simms confirmed that Michael Rossi was at the winery on Friday. He left around one o'clock that afternoon. He said he was surprised at the victim's sudden departure.'

'Didn't Rossi give any explanation as to why he was leaving early?'

'Apparently not, sir. Mr Simms said he'd spent the morning showing Michael Rossi the progress they were making with the harvest. After lunch, he left him in his study at the house to look for a spare set of house keys. When next he saw him, Michael Rossi announced he had to get back to Sydney.'

'Okay.'

'There's something else, sir,' said Reynolds. 'The barman at the Cruising Yacht Club has come forward to say the victim was at that club on Friday night and spoke at length with one of the other patrons. A man by the name of Robert Nesbit.'

'Oh? What time was this?' asked Fitzjohn.

'Around seven-thirty, sir.'

'Okay.' Fitzjohn swiveled his chair around to view the whiteboard as Williams stood aside. 'We've established that the victim left the winery at approximately one o'clock on Friday afternoon, presumably arriving back in Sydney around three. At 6pm, he entered his aunt's house in Waverton, and left around seven. At seven thirty, he entered the premises of the Cruising Yacht Club. So, where was he in the hours between three and six? We know he went home because his overnight bag was found in his study. The question is, was he there until he left for Esme Timmons's house? If he wasn't, I want to know where he was. See what you both can do. Oh, and first thing in the morning, find out what you can about Robert Nesbit.' Fitzjohn looked at his watch. 'But for now, I think you can call it a day.'

As the door closed behind the two officers, Fitzjohn picked up his pen and turned it end for end. His thoughts went through the day's events, culminating with Chief Superintendent Grieg, and his request for an audience. It was then the Incident Room door opened and Betts walked it. 'Ah, Betts, there you are. Any news?'

'I had a bit of luck, sir,' said Betts sitting down. 'I located Hannah Blair. Esme Timmons's cleaning lady. Apparently, she moved a couple of months ago and didn't think to tell Miss Timmons. I had her look through the rooms in the upper half of Miss Timmons's home and to her knowledge, there's nothing missing. Even so, I think it was probably difficult for her to tell under the circumstances.'

'Understandable,' said Fitzjohn, remembering the state of the room. 'I've just had Reynolds and Williams in here.' Fitzjohn relayed his meeting with the two officers. 'So, at least we now have a time line on the victim's movements yesterday. I've got them both working on the intervening three hours.' Fitzjohn sat forward. 'Let's turn our attention to what we have so far.'

Betts walked over to the whiteboard. 'Well, we have, Nigel Prentice, the victim's business partner who, it seems, has lied to us about when he left the council meeting last night. Pierce Whitehead, the victim's winemaker, who admits arguing with Michael Rossi the day before the murder. Then there's Charlotte Rossi, the victim's niece, who we now find has been joint owner of Five Oaks Winery since Claudia Rossi's death in 2010. Of course, it's still to be established whether Charlotte Rossi agreed or disagreed with the sale of the winery.'

'And a new player,' said Fitzjohn. 'Robert Nesbit, who was seen speaking to the victim at the Cruising Yacht Club not long before the victim died. He's also on the list of those people who tried to contact the victim earlier in the day on Friday. Who else is on that list, Betts?'

'Graeme Wyngard, sir.'

'Ah, yes, the owner of the yacht where, we believe, Rossi was attacked.'

'And Percy Green,' continued Betts. 'Apparently, he's an old school friend. When contacted, he said he was inviting Michael Rossi to an Old Boys dinner.'

Weary, Fitzjohn leant forward in his chair. 'Is that it?'

'Just one thing, sir. We recovered Claudia Rossi's 2010 diary on Wyngard's yacht.'

'Presumably the book Esme Timmons thought she saw Michael Rossi leave with on Friday night,' added Fitzjohn.

'Yes, but there's more. The slip of paper caught in the victim's fist may have been ripped from that diary. We'll know as soon as forensics has completed their examination.' Fitzjohn eyed his young sergeant with satisfaction.

'And what about Michael Rossi's diary. Anything interesting there?'

'Yes. The victim had made an appointment with his solicitor, David Spencer of Spencer, Anderson & Sumner, for this coming Monday afternoon.'

'Oh? Well in that case, we'll speak to Mr Spencer first thing in the morning to see if he knows what the appointment was to be about. Find out where we can find him on a Sunday morning, Betts. After that, we'll have a word with the victim's estranged wife. What was her name?'

'Stella Rossi, sir.'

Fitzjohn gathered his papers together. 'It's been a long day, Betts. We'll continue this tomorrow.'

'Can I give you a lift home, sir?'

'Fitzjohn thought for a moment. 'No. I'll get a taxi.'

The clock on the mantelpiece in the living room struck midnight as Fitzjohn opened the front door to his sandstone cottage in Birchgrove, and stepped inside. As he did so, he was met by a rush of hot air that had built up during the day's soaring heat and humidity. He placed his briefcase on the hall table, hung his suit coat on the end of the banister and turned on the air conditioning. Ten minutes later, now dressed in an old pair of slacks and an equally old T-shirt, Fitzjohn made his way outside again. This time into the back garden where he walked slowly down the path to the greenhouse. As he did so, he gazed up at the moon, its light filtering through the branches of a neighbour's tree, creating a soft glow. The cooling night air felt refreshing until he opened the greenhouse door and another rush of hot air hit him. Unperturbed, he switched on the light and surveyed the orchids standing silently in their rows before turning on the CD player that sat on the bench next to the door. With the sound of Mozart's Clarinet Concerto in A Major filling the air, Fitzjohn tended each orchid, the ashen face of Michael Rossi with his staring eyes, fading from his thoughts.

{CHAPTER 8}

Phillipa Braithwaite called to Charlotte who stood out on the patio. 'I've made some coffee.' Absentmindedly Charlotte looked around. 'I've put sugar in yours. I thought you could do with something sweet. It's good for shock. Or so I'm led to believe.' Phillipa placed the mugs on the glass-topped coffee table and sat down as Charlotte walked back inside.

'I can't believe Michael's gone.' Charlotte curled her legs up as she sat on the sofa and cradled her coffee mug in her hands. 'I know I complained about his controlling attitude a lot but, even so, I'll miss him.'

'Of course you will. Despite his recalcitrant behaviour, he was family after all.' Phillipa sipped her coffee. 'I was surprised, though, when I heard you tell the Chief Inspector that you'd agreed to be a referee for Pierce Whitehead. I thought you didn't like the man.'

'I don't. He's so... ingratiating.' Charlotte shivered. 'He unnerves me every time I speak to him.'

'So, why on earth did you agree to be his referee?'

'Because he's applying for a position in another State. Hopefully he'll be successful.' Charlotte looked at her watch. 'I wonder how long it'll be before the fridge arrives.'

'I don't know, but it's not necessary we both wait. Especially with what's happened. Why don't you go home and rest, Charlotte?'

'I can't Phil. I have to go over to see Esme. I just hope she hasn't found out what's happened to Michael from the morning news. And besides, you have the gallery to open at ten.'

'Trudy's agreed to do that. I phoned her while I was waiting for the coffee to perk. She's happy to fill in for me. For the whole day, if necessary. So, there's no reason for you stay. Go see to Esme. She'll need you.'

As she spoke the front door banged followed by footsteps on the marble floor in the front hall. Charlotte and Phillipa turned to see Stella Rossi.

'Stella!' said Charlotte, getting to her feet. 'Have you heard? About Michael.'

'Yes. It was on the early morning news,' Stella replied, her voice shaking. 'I drove straight to the marina but I couldn't get near the place, it's cordoned off, so I came here.' Stella pushed her hair away from her face and looked around in confusion.

'Why don't you sit down, Stella,' said Phillipa, 'and let me get you a cup of coffee. You look like you could do with one.'

'No, I couldn't drink a thing Phillipa. I just want to go home. I shouldn't have come here.'

Phillipa glanced at Charlotte.

'It might be best not to drive at the moment, Stella,' said Charlotte. 'You've had a terrible shock. Look. I was just about to go over to see Esme. Why don't I drive you home on my way? We can get your car back to you later today.'

Stella shook her head. 'No. It's okay, Charlotte. I can drive myself. I panicked, that's all.' Stella turned to go. 'Will you let me know when you hear anything? I know Michael and I were separated, but still, I...'

'Yes, of course,' replied Charlotte. 'As soon as I hear anything I'll let you know.'

After Stella left, Charlotte slumped back down on to the couch. 'Poor Stella. She's so distraught. And after everything that Michael put her through during their marriage. I guess she never really stopped loving him. I'm glad he didn't change his will after they separated. I think she deserves every penny she gets.'

'In that case Charlotte...' Charlotte's gaze followed Phillipa as she walked across the room and removed the sketch from the wall. 'I think you should take this with you when you leave here this morning. It's yours after all, and if it remains here it might be seen as part of Michael's estate.' Phillipa leant the sketch against the sofa. 'Not that I think Stella would make a fuss, but why complicate matters.'

'Mmm. You're probably right,' said Charlotte. 'I will take it...' The sound of the doorbell stopped Charlotte in mid-stream.

'That must be the fridge delivery,' said Phillipa. 'I'll go. Why don't you get yourself over to Esme's?'

Charlotte prepared to leave, oblivious to the voices coming from the front hall until Phillipa reappeared, followed by Robert Nesbit.

As a friend of her late father, John Merrell, Charlotte saw Robert Nesbit as a link to the father she had never known. Robert had been part of the crew on that fateful day, thirty years earlier, when a freak wave washed John Merrell into the sea. Now in his late fifties, his thick, fair hair peppered with grey, Robert Nesbit still competed in ocean yacht races, and continued to nurture Charlotte's interest in the sport, including her in his crew.

'Robert,' she said.

'I remembered you said you'd be here this morning, Charlotte, so I came as soon as I heard the news about Michael. I feel a bit awkward really, because I know Michael and I had our difficulties, but I felt the need to offer my condolences. Is there anything I can do?'

'No, I don't think so. But thanks for the offer. I'm just about to go over to see Esme. I'm hoping she hasn't heard about Michael's death on the news this morning. But I fear she will have. Would you like a cup of coffee? Phil just made a fresh pot.'

'Thanks, but no. I have a meeting at the Club in a few minutes. I just wanted to make sure you're all right. It's a difficult time, I know.' Robert half smiled. 'If you need anything, please don't hesitate.'

'Thanks, Robert. I'll see you out,' said Charlotte.

'He looks a lot older than I remember,' said Phillipa as Charlotte came back into the room.

'I know what you mean. I think it's because of what he's gone through in the last couple of years. It's such a shame. I don't think he ever fully recovered from his wife's affair with Michael and the subsequent collapse of the business. I hate to say it, Phil, but I think Michael ruined Robert Nesbit's life.'

***

Charlotte walked between the two vans parked in front of Esme's home, both displaying the word forensics. With a sense of urgency, she opened the garden gate and hurried along the cracked cement path to the front door. After knocking twice, the door opened and Esme appeared.

'Oh, Charlotte, my dear. I'm glad you're here. Come in.' Esme shut the door behind her. 'I was a bit worried I might have missed you while I was out.'

'Have you heard, Esme?'

'About Michael? Yes, on the news early this morning.' Esme took a small handkerchief from her pocket and dabbed her nose. Charlotte put her arms around Esme's diminutive frame.

'I'm sorry I didn't get here sooner.' As Charlotte spoke, the sound of voices came from upstairs.

'Who's up there, Esme?'

'It's the police, dear. I think they call themselves SOCOs. Short for Scene of Crime Officers. They're gathering evidence.'

Charlotte's brow furrowed. 'For what?'

'It's because of last night's break-in. Come through to the kitchen and I'll tell you all about it.'

'Esme?' Charlotte shot a look up the stairwell before following Esme through the house. 'You did say break-in, didn't you?'

'Yes, I did. It was just after two o'clock this morning.' Esme filled the kettle with water, put it down on the stove, and turned on the gas. 'The police are here to try to establish whether there's any connection between the break-in and Michael's... and what happened to Michael. He was here last night, you see.'

Charlotte sat down heavily at the kitchen table and looked aghast at Esme. 'How can you be so cool about this, Esme?'

'I'm not cool. I just look cool,' answered Esme. 'Actually, I'm a mess. And I need a cup of tea.'

'I'll make it,' said Charlotte, jumping up. 'You sit down.'

'So, Michael came here last night,' continued Charlotte bringing the tea to the table.

'Yes, he dropped in around six. When he left, he said he was going over to see you. Didn't he do that?'

'I don't know. I didn't close the bookshop till nine, so it was quite late by the time I got home.'

'Oh, that's unfortunate. I had hoped he might have told you why he was looking for letters in your mother's study.'

'You've lost me Esme,' said Charlotte, sitting down again at the table.

'It's what Michael came here for. At least that's what he said. To finds some letters in your mother's study.' Esme took a sip of her tea. 'The intruder was in there too. I know because I saw him coming out of that room. And that's why I was out this morning. I went to Kings Cross Police Station to see the detective who's in charge of the investigation. Detective Chief Inspector Fitzjohn is his name. A very fine man. Reminded me a bit of my cousin, Selwyn.'

Charlotte looked in disbelief at Esme. 'How did you get to Kings Cross?'

'On the train,' said Esme between sips of her tea. 'I thought it'd be the best mode of transport, and it was other than the fact the train from Town Hall didn't have any air conditioning. I was a bit parched by the time I got to the police station.'

'Oh, Esme. I wish you'd phoned me. I could have driven you there.'

'I suppose you could. I never thought. It was one of those spur of the moment things.' Esme sat thoughtfully. 'Poor Michael. What a dreadful thing to have happen to him.' They both sat for a few moments in silence.

'I can't understand why Michael came back from the winery early,' said Charlotte, at last. 'He told me on Friday morning that he planned to spend the whole weekend there.'

'Really? Well, that's unusual in itself, isn't it. He never liked spending more than a day at a time at the winery. He said the place reminded him of your mother.'

'It did, but this weekend he had a specific purpose in mind,' said Charlotte. 'He was having Five Oaks Winery listed on the property market.'

'*Selling the winery?*' Esme slumped back in her chair. 'And were you happy about that, Charlotte? After all, the place is half yours.'

'No, I wasn't, but I couldn't afford to buy Michael out so I didn't have any choice but to go along with it. He wanted the money to finance the take-over of his business in Rushcutters Bay. He wanted, his partner, Nigel Prentice, out. But I think he had another reason as well. I think he saw selling the winery as a way for him to deal with Mum's death. You know what difficulty he had accepting what happened to her. The winery was just another reminder. Her influence was everywhere.'

'Mmm. You could be right,' said Esme. 'He never did get over your mother's death. Perhaps it had something to do with her being his twin.'

'I don't know,' said Charlotte, 'but what I do know is, we all had difficulty at the time, and it irritated me that Michael went on so about it. It only made things worse.' Esme patted Charlotte's hand. 'Anyway, Esme, let's get back to what matters now. Are you all right, and was anything taken in the home invasion?'

'I'm fine, dear, but it's hard to tell whether there's anything missing. The room's in such a mess.'

'Well, when the police have finished I'll help you put it right. And, if you don't mind, I'd like to stay with you for a few nights. I don't like the thought of you being here on your own.' Charlotte smiled. 'I know if I ask you to come and stay with me you'd say no.'

'You're right. I would.' Esme smiled. 'I know I'm incorrigible, but I do like to sleep in my own bed. Having you stay, however, would make me feel easier.'

'Good. Then that's settled.' Charlotte looked at her watch. 'It's a bit late in the day now to fetch my things so I'll do that in the morning.'

❃CHAPTER 9❃

The sparrows, splashing in the birdbath, did not distract Fitzjohn as he surveyed his garden early the next morning. They only added to his pleasure along with the flowerbeds yielding an abundance of colour and fragrances. Lamenting the fact he could not spend his Sunday morning pottering in this peaceful place, Fitzjohn turned and made his way back into the house. As he did so, he heard his niece's voice as she came through the front door.

'Hello, anybody home?' When she reached the kitchen doorway, Sophie stopped. 'Oh, hello, Uncle Alistair. It looks like you're ready to go out.'

'Duty calls, I'm afraid.' Fitzjohn adjusted the handkerchief in the breast pocket of his suit coat. 'But to what do I owe this surprise visit so early on a Sunday morning, young lady?'

'I came to borrow a thermos. I seem to remember seeing one in your laundry cupboard when I was house-sitting last month.'

'I didn't know I had a thermos,' said Fitzjohn. 'Your Aunt Edith took care of all that kind of thing. But you're welcome to look. Are you going on a picnic?'

'No, Uncle. I'm going to a sit-in at the university. I want to take a hot drink along in case we're there all night.' Fitzjohn's eyes narrowed. Since his sister, Meg, had allowed Sophie to continue her university studies in Sydney rather than Melbourne, Fitzjohn had felt a certain sense of responsibility toward his young niece. He also sensed that the move was Sophie's way of escaping her mother's overbearing grasp. Could he blame her? Ever since Edith's death, he had experienced that overbearing grasp first hand.

'What kind of sit-in is it, Sophie? You know that sort of thing can turn ugly.'

Sophie smiled. 'You don't need to worry, Uncle Alistair, it's just a campus matter to do with one of the libraries.' Sophie made a quick exit into the laundry room, and amidst the clatter of her emptying the cupboard, Betts arrived.

'I thought you might like a lift, sir.' Betts looked around as another crash sounded. 'What's that? Mice?'

'No, it's Sophie. She's looking for something in the laundry.' Fitzjohn moved over to the kitchen table and commenced placing papers into his briefcase. Just then, Sophie reappeared, her face lighting up when she spied Betts.

'Oh, Martin. Just the person I wanted to see. I've just this minute found your running shoes in the laundry cupboard. The ones that got soaked the night you helped me with the greenhouse.'

Fitzjohn eyed Betts suspiciously as Sophie darted back into the laundry, and reappeared with the shoes. She handed them to Betts.

'Did you find the thermos, Sophie?' asked Fitzjohn.

'Not yet, but I'm sure it's there.'

'Then lock up when you leave and mind what I said. Sit-ins can get ugly.'

'I will, Uncle Alistair,' she answered while smiling at Betts. 'It's lovely to see you again, Martin.'

Carrying his shoes, Betts looked back over his shoulder and smiled as he and Fitzjohn left.

'I thought I made it clear that my niece is off limits, Betts,' said Fitzjohn when they reached the car.

'You did, sir. And it is… clear, that it.'

'Then can you tell me why you were here, with Sophie, while I was away in England? And why your shoes were in my laundry cupboard.' Fitzjohn glared at Betts over the car roof.

'I came over to help Sophie with the greenhouse. I must have left my shoes... behind.' Betts's voice tapered off. 'It's not the way it sounds… exactly. You see, while you were away, we had a storm. A bad storm. Hail stones, the lot. One of the panes of glass in your greenhouse broke and Sophie rang and asked me if I could fix it.'

'And you said yes? What do you know about installing glass?'

'I don't, and I didn't. I just sealed it up with green garbage bags and masking tape until Sophie could get someone out to replace it the next day. She was concerned about the orchids, sir. She had visions of them all being destroyed by the time you got home.'

'That doesn't explain why you left your shoes behind.'

'Oh, I can explain that too, sir. You see, they got soaked while I was out there putting the plastic over the break in the glass. Later, I took them off while Sophie made me a hot drink. She gave me a pair of yours to wear home.'

Fitzjohn grimaced. 'You *wore* a pair of my shoes? A better question. How did you manage to get your large feet into a pair of my shoes?'

'It wasn't easy,' said Betts. 'In the end, I gave up and Sophie gave me a pair of your rubber boots. A green pair. I've still got them. I'll return them tomorrow.'

'See that you do, Sergeant.' Skeptical that he had been told the whole story, but at the same time amused, Fitzjohn got into the car. 'Be warned, Betts. Sophie is far too young for you. She's barely twenty years old.'

'You're right, sir. She is. Too young. For me, that is.'

'Good, I'm glad you agree. Now, I want to turn our attention to Michael Rossi's solicitor.' Fitzjohn pulled his seat belt on.

'Before we do, sir, a couple of things have turned up. Firstly, other than the phone calls that we know Michael Rossi received on the day of his death, he also received one from his estranged wife, Stella Rossi. And judging from the time of the call, he would have just arrived back in Sydney.'

'So, we can dismiss the idea that her call had any bearing on him leaving the winery earlier than planned. What else, Betts?'

'I ran a check on Pierce Whitehead, sir. Apparently, he lives in South Africa.'

'*What?*'

'He has done for the past six years.'

A stunned look on his face, Fitzjohn said, 'So who's the man purporting to be our winemaker?'

'I've got Williams working on it, sir. He's trying to contact the real Mr Whitehead to see if he's able to identify our imposter.'

'Good. In the meantime, where can we find Michael Rossi's solicitor on a Sunday morning?'

'At his home in Lavender Bay, sir. I called ahead. He's expecting us.'

<hr />

A short, lean man opened the door, his tousled brown hair dipping over his forehead. In his mid-to-late-thirties, and younger than Fitzjohn had envisaged, he wore a T-shirt displaying the Eiffel Tower along with a pair of beige coloured shorts, cut off just below his knees. Fitzjohn and Betts showed their warrant cards.

'Good morning, gentlemen. I'm David Spencer. I've been expecting you. Please, come in.' Fitzjohn and Betts followed David Spencer through a chaotic atmosphere filled with a screaming baby and two small boys arguing over a television remote. 'You'll have to excuse the racket. The delights of family life, I'm afraid. Pandemonium for the greater part of the time.' He chuckled to himself and opened the door into a room overlooking a small courtyard. 'We can talk in my study undisturbed. The walls are sound proofed.' As David Spencer closed the door behind them, Fitzjohn and Betts settled themselves into the two rounded leather chairs in front of the solicitor's desk. 'I understand you've come to see me about Michael Rossi,' he said, sitting down behind his desk. 'How exactly can I help?'

'According to Michael Rossi's diary, Mr Spencer,' began Fitzjohn, 'Michael Rossi was to have an appointment with you this coming Monday morning. Can you tell us what the appointment was to be about?

'Yes. He said he wanted to speak to me about his will, but on Friday afternoon, Mr Rossi rang to cancel Monday's appointment and asked if he could come in to see me here at the house on Saturday instead.' David Spencer's brow furrowed. 'I was preparing for that appointment yesterday morning when I heard the news of his death. A terrible business,' said Spencer, shaking his head.

'What time on Friday did he phone, Mr Spencer?' asked Fitzjohn.

'He phoned my office in North Sydney around four o'clock in the afternoon, as I remember.'

'Did he give any indication as to why he wanted to change the day of his appointment?'

'No. But he did say he wanted to speak to me about another matter as well as his will.'

'Oh?'

'Yes. He said he wanted to discuss his sister, Claudia Rossi. He didn't go into specifics, but he did say he wanted advice about her life insurance policy. Consequently, when Sergeant Betts telephoned earlier this morning, I made a point of not only getting a copy of Mr Rossi's will out of safe custody, but also Claudia Rossi's. Under the circumstances, I thought there was every possibility you'd want to see them both.' Spencer took Claudia's will out of its long thin envelope.

'Does this tell us who she was insured with?' asked Fitzjohn running his eyes across the document.

'Yes. On the second page.' Fitzjohn turned to the next page. 'As you can see. It was with the MLC for the sum of one million dollars.'

'And the beneficiary?'

'Her partner, Richard Edwards with Michael Rossi as contingent beneficiary. That is, Mr Rossi would receive the benefit if the primary designee had been unavailable or deceased.'

'I see. May we take Claudia Rossi's will with us, Mr Spencer?'

'By all means.' Spencer handed Fitzjohn the will's envelope. 'And as far as Michael Rossi's will is concerned, I take it you want to know who the beneficiary is there too,' said David Spencer.

'There's only one?' asked Fitzjohn.

'Yes.' Spencer unfolded Michael Rossi's will and laid it out in front of Fitzjohn and Betts. 'I read through it before you arrived. The bulk of Mr Rossi's estate goes to his wife Stella Rossi. It comprises all monies, shares, debenture stocks as well as the property in Rushcutters Bay and Michael Rossi's share of the business, Rossi & Prentice Yachting Electronics Pty Ltd.'

'So he didn't change his will after he and his wife separated,' said Fitzjohn.

'No.'

'Tell me, Mr Spencer, is Stella Rossi aware of this?'

'Yes. Michael had me write to her not long after their separation, telling her that he had no plans to make any changes to his will. He never asked me to write a letter contradicting that.'

'Mmm.' Fitzjohn rubbed his chin before he continued. 'We understand that Michael Rossi also owned half share in a winery in the Hunter Valley.'

'That's correct. Five Oaks Winery. The will stipulates that it's to be inherited by his sister, Claudia Rossi, but if she predeceases him, it goes to her daughter, Charlotte Rossi, which is, of course, what will happen.'

'And is Charlotte Rossi aware of this?'

'That I can't say, Chief Inspector, but being that the winery has passed down through the Rossi family from her great-grandparents, I should imagine she does.'

———

Fitzjohn and Betts returned to their car, Fitzjohn settling himself into the passenger seat. His gaze went the full length of Walker Street to where Sydney's CBD shimmered in the heat like a mirage over the harbour, his thoughts, however, were elsewhere. 'I wonder if the letters Michael Rossi was looking for at Esme Timmons's residence on Friday night were to do with Claudia Rossi's life insurance policy, Betts. And if that's the case, I wonder what sparked his interest.'

Betts shrugged as he started the car. 'Surely the policy has been paid out by now, sir.'

'Nevertheless, I want you to contact the insurance company and find out exactly when it was paid. But before you do that, we'll speak to Nigel Prentice again. I'm interested to hear how he explains where he was after eight o'clock on Friday evening. And then there's Charlotte Rossi. We'll pay her a call as well to find out how she felt about her uncle selling the winery.'

'You mean if she didn't agree with the sale she had a pretty strong motive to kill Michael Rossi.'

'If she knew she'd inherit his share; yes, I do, Betts.'

———

Fitzjohn's knock on Nigel Prentice's front door was answered by a short, plump woman in her early fifties. 'Are you collecting for the Salvos,' she asked with an engaging smile.

'No, madam. We're from the New South Wales Police.' Fitzjohn held up his warrant card. 'I'm Detective Chief Inspector Fitzjohn and this is Detective Sergeant Betts.'

'Oh. I beg your pardon. Nigel did say he'd spoken to the police yesterday. I'm Maggie Prentice. Nigel's wife. Please, come in, Chief Inspector. It's shocking about poor Michael,' she continued. 'Seems nobody's safe these days. If you'd care to wait in there,' she gestured to the living room, 'I'll go fetch Nigel. He's out the back.'

As Mrs Prentice disappeared, Fitzjohn and Betts circled the living room, taking in its 1980s flare. Minutes passed before Nigel Prentice appeared, brushing his clothes down. 'Sorry to keep you waiting gentlemen. I was doing a bit of gardening. Won't you have a seat?'

'We have a few more questions,' said Fitzjohn, sitting down. 'We'd like to know where you were after you left the council meeting on the night Michael Rossi died.'

'But I explained that yesterday, Chief Inspector.' Prentice sat down on the sofa. 'I came straight home.'

'So you said. The only problem is, a gentleman who attended the same council meeting said you left that meeting around eight o'clock. And as you said you arrived home at ten, I wonder if you can tell us where you were in those two intervening hours. That is, between eight and ten.'

With beads of perspiration appearing on his forehead, Prentice jumped up from his chair and closed the living room door. Returning to his seat, he clasped his hands together and whispered, 'I met a friend, Chief Inspector.'

'A friend?' repeated Fitzjohn.

'Yes. A woman friend, if you get my meaning.' Prentice's eyes darted toward the closed door.

'Oh, I do,' answered Fitzjohn. 'Can we have your friend's name?' Fitzjohn waited for Prentice to reply. 'It could cause you problems if you don't tell us, Mr Prentice, because we might assume you were not with a friend at all, but at your place of business during the time of Michael Rossi's murder.'

'But that absurd.'

'Then where were you, and who were you with?' asked Fitzjohn again, his impatience growing.

Prentice fidgeted with the crocheted doily on the arm of the sofa. 'All right. I was with Stella Rossi. After the council meeting finished we met up and we went for a drive. Up the north shore. Colloroy way. I hope this doesn't have to go any further, Chief Inspector. I'm sure you'll understand. My wife, you see…'

'Oh, I understand only too well,' said Fitzjohn.

'I wonder if teaming up with Stella Rossi was a strategic move on Nigel Prentice's part,' said Betts, getting into the car a few minutes later. 'I mean, he could see it as a way of gaining control of the company.'

'You mean by persuading Mrs Rossi to let him run it?'

'Yes, sir.'

'Sounds logical, but if he's that devious, do you really believe he'd be satisfied with only owning half the shares?'

'No. Probably not,' replied Betts, 'but one thing's for sure. Nigel Prentice and Stella Rossi both had motive to murder Michael Rossi because between the two of them they now own Rossi & Prentice Yachting Electronics, outright.'

'They do, Betts. But whether they had the means and opportunity to kill Michael Rossi, remains to be seen.' Fitzjohn looked at his watch. 'And while we're figuring that out let's have another word with Charlotte Rossi.'

{CHAPTER 10}

G one was the infectious smile on Charlotte Rossi's face, so visible the previous day. Instead, she appeared tense when she opened the door to her apartment.

'Chief Inspector.'

'Ms Rossi, our apologies for disturbing your Sunday, but we'd like to speak to you again if we may.' Charlotte eyes darted from Fitzjohn to Betts and back to Fitzjohn.

'By all means,' she said, stepping back from the doorway. 'Come in. Do you have news about my uncle?'

'No, not yet,' answered Fitzjohn, 'but there are a few unanswered questions we thought you might be able to help us with.'

'I hope I can,' she said as she led the way along a short hallway and into a sun-filled living room. 'What is it you want to ask?'

'I seem to remember you said the last time you spoke to your uncle was on Friday morning,' said Fitzjohn, sitting down.

'That's right. He came here to drop off his house keys so that I could take delivery of the fridge.'

'So you didn't see him after that? Miss Timmons seems to think he planned to call around after he'd left her place.'

'Mmm. Esme mentioned that yesterday, but as I think I told you before, Chief Inspector, I worked late on Friday night. I didn't get home until after nine. So, I don't know whether he called around or not.'

'Did he try to contact you by phone?'

'There was a missed call on my mobile, but when I rang him back, there was no reply.' Charlotte's brow furrowed. 'By that time he was probably... Oh God.'

Fitzjohn waited for a moment before he continued his questioning. 'Can you think of anyone who would want to harm your uncle, Ms Rossi?'

'He wasn't popular with a number of people, Chief Inspector, but I wouldn't have thought that their grievances would go as far as murder.'

'Can you tell us who these people were?' When Charlotte Rossi did not reply, Fitzjohn continued. 'For instance. What do you know about a man called Percy Greene?'

'Percy? He's... He was an acquaintance of Michael's. An old school friend. Percy handles the Old Boys network, but that's all I know about him.'

'What about Graeme Wyngard.'

'Wyngard. I believe he was a client of Michael's. I've had some dealings with him when I've worked in Michael's office. Rather a pompous sort. Full of himself, if you know what I mean.'

'And Robert Nesbit?'

'Robert? I've known Robert all my life, Chief Inspector. He and my father were friends. They sailed together. Robert Nesbit was there when my father was lost at sea.' Charlotte paused. 'I'm also part of Robert's crew. Once upon a time, he and Michael were friends as well as business partners until...'

'Until what, Ms Rossi?'

'Oh. Something happened... they fell out and Michael left the business.'

'Can you tell us what happened?' Charlotte Rossi remained silent. 'If you know anything at all Ms Rossi...'

'Well, I suppose you'll find out eventually.' Charlotte sighed. 'The truth of the matter is, Michael had an affair with Robert's wife. It broke up Robert's marriage.'

Betts looked up from his notebook.

'I see,' said Fitzjohn. 'And I take it this also led to the end of their business partnership.'

'Yes. It did.'

'When did this happen?' asked Fitzjohn.

'Just over two years ago. At the beginning of 2010.'

'And your uncle's marriage?'

'It collapsed too. He and Stella separated soon after.'

'I'm told they never divorced.'

'No, they didn't. As far as I know, Stella never asked for a divorce and Michael didn't offer. To tell you the truth, I think he hoped that one day Stella would come back to him.' After a moment, Charlotte looked at her watch.

'I don't want to keep you too long, Ms Rossi, but I do have a couple more questions. The first being Five Oaks Winery. We understand you have a 50 percent share.'

'Yes, my mother left it to me in her will.'

'So, were you in agreement when your uncle decided to sell?'

Charlotte fingered the gold chain around her neck. 'No, I wasn't, but I couldn't afford to buy Michael out so there wasn't much I could do about it.'

Fitzjohn sensed Charlotte Rossi's growing restiveness. 'Did you voice your disapproval to your uncle?'

'Of course. Several times. The last time being on Friday morning when he came by to drop off his keys. He wanted to make sure I'd agree to sign the listing agreement.'

'And did you? Agree, that is.'

'Yes, because I knew there was no point in arguing with Michael. He'd just have kept wearing me down until he got his way.'

'And what about now that your uncle's... gone?'

With a pinched expression, Charlotte Rossi met Fitzjohn's intense gaze. 'If you're referring to the winery's ownership, Chief Inspector, I'll inherit Michael's share. It's always been passed down through my family. Unless, of course, Michael made other arrangements in his will.' Charlotte Rossi looked at her watch again. 'Will this take much longer? It's just that...'

Fitzjohn looked over to the suitcase on the dining room table. 'Are you going away, Ms Rossi?' he asked.

'I stayed with my Aunt Esme last night. I was worried about her being alone after the break-in. I plan to stay with her for the next few days so I came home for a few things.' Charlotte paused. 'Do you think that the break-in had something to do with Michael's death, Chief Inspector?'

'That depends on whether your uncle and the person who broke into your aunt's house on Friday night were looking for the same thing, Ms Rossi. Apparently, your uncle told Miss Timmons he was looking for letters. We haven't been able to establish whether he found them or not.'

'My second question, Ms Rossi,' continued Fitzjohn, 'is about Nigel Prentice. In as much as how he and your uncle got along.'

'They got along fine until just recently.'

'Oh? Do you know what happened to change that?'

'I'm not sure, but I suspect it might have something to do with what Michael told me a few weeks ago. That he planned to buy Nigel out of the business. I think that was one of the reasons he wanted to sell the winery. To raise cash. I don't know how, but Nigel must have got wind of Michael's plans.' Charlotte thought for a moment. 'I know my uncle would have preferred to own the business outright from the start, Chief Inspector, but obviously he couldn't afford to at the time.'

'So would I be right in saying he found it equally difficult to have a winemaker managing the winery?' asked Fitzjohn. 'It's just that I seem to remember you said there was a problem there too. With Pierce Whitehead, that is.'

'Mmm. Michael never liked Pierce. Of course, it didn't matter when my mother was alive because Michael didn't have anything to do with the winery. Mum was Pierce's immediate contact. But nothing went smoothly after she died because Michael and Pierce clashed.'

'Is Mr Whitehead difficult to get along with?'

'Not especially.'

'What do you know about his past, Ms Rossi?'

'Only what my mother told me. Before he came to us, he'd spent six years in France.'

'And before that?'

'I have no idea.'

'Do you know how your mother came to employ him?' Charlotte's hand went back to the gold chain around her neck.

'No. She never said, and I didn't ask. She would have thought me meddlesome.' Charlotte paused. 'My mother didn't like to be questioned about her decisions, Chief Inspector. I suppose in that respect, she was very much like Michael.' Charlotte gave a quick smile.

'Very well, Ms Rossi. We won't keep you any longer.'

———

'So,' said Fitzjohn, as Betts put the car into gear and pulled away from the curb, 'Charlotte Rossi did believe that, in the event of her uncle's death, she would more than likely end up the sole owner of the winery. And in light of the fact that he was about to sell the place, it does give her a strong motive to kill Michael Rossi.'

'Unlikely though. Wouldn't you say, sir?'

'Why, Betts?'

'Because she doesn't weigh more than a feather. I don't see how she could...'

'I admit she's slight, Betts, but she's also fit, not to mention familiar with the workings of yachts. And then there's the possibility she had help.'

'Who by?'

'Pierce Whitehead,' said Fitzjohn, adjusting his wire-framed glasses. 'After all, they both had something to gain.'

'But she says she hardly knows the man.'

'So she did. And very convincingly too. But do you believe her?'

———

Later that same day, Fitzjohn walked into Day Street Police Station to greetings from his fellow officers. Wanting to get his meeting with Chief Superintendent Grieg over as quickly as possible, he wasted no time in reaching Grieg's office where he felt the tension in the air as soon as he entered.

'You took your damn time,' said Grieg, tossing his pen aside.

'I'm sorry about that, sir. It couldn't be helped.' Fitzjohn sighed, digging deep for patience, and the ability to be civil to Grieg.

Grieg sat back in his chair making a steeple with his fingers while he studied Fitzjohn. 'I don't want your excuses,' he spat. 'I called you here because I understand your investigations have led you to interview a man by the name of Wyngard.'

His interest piqued, Fitzjohn answered, 'Yes, they have. The victim died on Graeme Wyngard's yacht. Why? Is there a problem, Chief Superintendent?'

Grieg's hands went to the arms of his chair as he glared at Fitzjohn. 'Mr Wyngard has lodged a complaint concerning your discourteous behaviour toward him.'

'I'm aware of that,' said Fitzjohn. 'He lodged it at Kings Cross Police Station on Saturday afternoon because I refused to release his yacht.' A slight smiled crossed over Fitzjohn's face. 'I understand he's missed his yacht race today.'

'Release the damn yacht Fitzjohn,' barked Grieg. 'Immediately.'

'I will. When we have no further use of it... sir.' Grieg's face reddened.

'Don't push me Fitzjohn, because you'll regret it.'

As Sunday night closed in, Fitzjohn returned to Kings Cross Police Station, feeling unsettled. Did Grieg have a mole at Kings Cross, keeping tabs on him and his investigation? What else could explain how Grieg knew about Wyngard's complaint? With this thought playing on his mind, he opened the Incident Room door to find Williams at one of the desks. 'It's late Williams. Don't you have a home to go to?'

'I'm just finishing up my notes, sir.'

Fitzjohn sat heavily into his chair, surprised at Williams's dedication to duty. A far cry from the Williams he had known at Day Street Station. Why the change, he wondered. Was it due to Williams getting away from Day Street and Chief Superintendent Grieg? Didn't Williams mention that he had been permanently moved at Grieg's request? Or was that a well engineered story? Was Williams Grieg's mole?

❧CHAPTER 11❧

The drone of cicadas filled the hot afternoon air as Charlotte returned to Esme's. Letting herself into the house, she placed her overnight bag, along with the sketch, next to the staircase in the front hall, and walked through to the kitchen. 'Esme. I'm back. I just...' Reaching the doorway Charlotte stopped. The room stood empty, the monotonous drip of the tap into the stainless steel sink breaking the silence and adding a sense of abandonment. Charlotte turned back, retracing her steps. As she reached Esme's bedroom door, she tapped lightly. 'Esme, are you there?' she asked. The door swung open and Charlotte's heart quickened. An old photo album lay on the floor, its contents strewn across the room. With growing uneasiness, she returned to the front hall and called again. 'Esme?'

'I'm up here, dear,' came Esme's soft voice from above.

With relief, Charlotte raced up the stairs to find her great-aunt sitting in a chair in the study. 'Oh, Esme. I thought...'

'What is it, dear? You look flustered.'

'I just found your photo album on the floor in your bedroom and...'

'Oh, yes, I dropped it and with it being so old, the pages fell out. Then the phone rang and I got distracted.'

Charlotte picked her way through the papers scattered across the study floor and perched herself on the edge of the desk. 'I thought you didn't come upstairs anymore Esme.'

'I don't usually, but it's not every day one's house is burgled. I wanted to have another look to see if anything's missing. But then I sat down and started reminiscing instead. I loved it when your mother spent time in here.' Esme smiled in reflection. 'She hummed while she worked, you know. At that time, I slept in one of the bedrooms up here, and I used to listen to her. I found it comforting.' Esme paused. 'But, enough of my musings,' she said, casting her eyes around. 'This room's a mess, isn't it?'

'Yes, it is, but I'll have it tidied up in no time. You'll see.' Charlotte bent down and started picking up papers and books from the floor. 'I'd have been back sooner, but I got delayed by the police.'

'Oh. Did they have news?' asked Esme, her eyes lighting up.

'No, they just asked me a lot of questions about the people who knew Michael. And about the winery. They seemed particularly interested in the fact that I'm part owner, and wanted to know how I felt about Michael selling the place.' Charlotte looked up at Esme. 'I got an uncomfortable feeling that they think I could have something to do with his death.' Esme leaned forward and patted Charlotte's shoulder.

'They're just doing their job, dear. And to do that, they have to look at every possibility. Don't let it worry you.' Esme smiled.

'Look on the bright side. You won't have to sell the winery now because you'll own it out-right.'

Charlotte placed the papers she had gathered on to the desk.

'Well, that may or may not be the case, Esme.'

'Whatever do you mean?'

'I mean that there's every possibility Michael left his share of the winery to Stella.'

'To Stella? Why on earth would he do that? Surely he made a new will when his marriage to Stella collapsed. And even if he didn't. It was always understood that you'd inherit the winery.'

'Well, I know Stella is the sole beneficiary of Michael's estate which is as it should be. But whether or not that includes the winery, I don't know. We'll just have to wait until the will is made available.'

'And in the meantime?' asked Esme.

'I thought I'd drive up to Five Oaks tomorrow. With what's happened, I think I should speak to Rafe Simms. He's completing the harvest since Pierce Whitehead quit.'

'I didn't know that Pierce quit,' replied Esme in surprise. 'What happened?'

'Apparently, he and Michael argued. It was right in the middle of harvest. I'm surprised Michael didn't mention it to you, Esme.'

'No. Not a word. But it doesn't surprise me. Michael wasn't one for sharing anything. And as for the argument. I can't think of anyone Michael got along with for long. Can you?'

'Only Rafe Simms. I think Michael respected Rafe. And thank goodness he did because not only is Rafe finishing the harvest, but he's buying the grapes at an agreed price.'

'And if the winery is left to you. What will you do?'

'I'll have to make some quick decisions about its management, I suppose,' answered Charlotte.

'You could always put your degree in viticulture to good use and manage it yourself.'

Charlotte shook her head. 'I don't think so, Esme. I can't see myself ever living at Five Oaks Winery now.'

'A bit too close is it? To Rafe Simms.'

'Yes. It is.'

Esme sat back again in her chair. 'You know, despite your mother's opinion of him, I always liked Rafe. He reminds me very much of his grandfather. A handsome man if there ever was one. If I hadn't been engaged to Thomas at the time…' Esme's eyes sparkled.

Charlotte bent down again and gathered up more papers, wanting to avoid any further conversation about Rafe that would cause her to revisit the past.

'You know, Esme, I've been thinking,' she said, in an attempt to put Rafe to the back of her mind. 'Michael would never have left the winery without first listing the property with the real estate agent unless it was something dire.'

'I agree,' said Esme. 'And I think it had something to do with your mother because when he arrived here on Friday evening, he was like a man possessed. All he wanted to do was come straight up to this room.' Esme got to her feet, steadying herself on the desk. 'That's odd,'

'What is it?' asked Charlotte.

'The perfume bottle is gone. It always sat here.' Esme's hand trembled as it touched the surface of the bureau.

Charlotte sensed Esme's deep disappointment. 'I'm so sorry, Esme.'

'So am I, Charlotte. Not because it was worth a great deal, but because it was one of my treasures. It belonged to my grandmother.' Esme sighed. 'I suppose the police should be told. It could mean that the break-in wasn't connected to Michael's death.' Esme wrapped her cardigan around herself. 'Either way, I think I'll go downstairs and make us both some tea,' she said.

Charlotte watched Esme leave the study, appreciating that the perfume bottle's disappearance was just one too many blows for Esme. Kneeling down again, she picked up the remaining papers and books from the floor and placed them on the desk before reaching to close the desk drawer. It was then she noticed an envelope wedged in the back of the drawer. Using a ruler, she nudged it out before removing its contents. The heading caught her eye. "Report into the provenance of the Brandt sketch". Charlotte settled herself into the chair and flipped through the report. It was then she heard Esme calling.

'Coming,' she replied. Charlotte closed the desk drawer and left the room, taking the report with her. She found Esme at the kitchen table pouring the tea.

'Did you find something, after all?' asked Esme, seeing the papers in Charlotte's hand.

'Yes. It's a report Mum was preparing on a sketch she purchased in 2010.'

'Not the one that's sitting in the front hall next to your overnight bag.'

'Yes, as a matter of fact.' Charlotte laid the report out on the table. 'I'd forgotten I'd left it in my car yesterday when I got here.'

'Your mother showed that sketch to me just after she'd bought it. I can't say it's to my taste.'

'Nor mine, Esme. That's why I lent it to Michael. He loved it. And I must admit, it did fit in well with the décor of his house. It's by a well known artist called Brandt.'

'Yes, I know. Arthur Brandt. He was featured on a television show I watched not long ago. One of those SBS shows on art.' Esme sipped her tea while Charlotte gazed at the report. 'It never ceases to amaze me that many of the most sought after pieces of artwork are not pleasing to the eye. At least not mine. And this report is about its provenance, you say?'

'Yes. Which seems odd because I can't imagine Mum buying anything without its provenance being in-tact, or at least being satisfied with it. Can you, Esme?'

'No. That's where your mother and Michael were alike. Fastidious about detail. What does the report conclude?'

Charlotte flipped through the pages. 'It's not finished so there's no conclusion. But Mum does have notes here, at the end, about what she plans to do the following week. The week of July 11th, 2010.'

Esme gasped. 'The week your mother passed away.'

'Yes.' Charlotte paused. 'It's such a shame she was never able to finish this.'

'Why don't you do it for her, dear? That way your mother's work will be complete, and as the owner of the sketch, you'll be assured of its provenance.'

'It sounds like a good idea, Esme, but I don't know that I have the expertise. I know nothing about art or who to approach.'

'What about your mother's notes? You could start there.'

'I suppose so. I'll read through them again, and think about it.' Charlotte sat back and cradled her cup in her hands. 'Would you like to come to the winery with me tomorrow, Esme? It'll make for a nice change.'

'You know, I think I'd like that. It's been a long time since I've been to the Hunter Valley.'

Charlotte smiled. 'Then it's settled. We'll plan on leaving late morning, after I've been into the bookshop. I need to let Irene know that I'll be away.'

{CHAPTER 12}

Early the next morning, Betts arrived at Fitzjohn's
Birchgrove home to find his boss in the back garden
looking upward to a tree branch hanging precariously
over the greenhouse. 'Good morning, sir.'

Fitzjohn turned. 'Betts. I thought you had a meeting with the
insurance company this morning.'

'It's not till eleven,' said Betts, following Fitzjohn's intent gaze
to the branch swaying in the wind. 'That whole tree needs taking
down, sir.'

'If you can convince my neighbour of that fact, Betts, I'll give
you a medal.'

'I take it you've spoken to him about it, sir.'

'It's not a him, Betts, it's a rather formidable woman by the
name of Rhonda Butler. And yes, we've had words. On several
occasions. But it hasn't done any good. She refuses to take any
action because the tree provides her house and garden with shade
throughout the summer months.' Fitzjohn lifted his eyebrows.

'Nevertheless, I think you're within your rights to, at least, have that branch removed, sir.'

'I know. In fact, I rang the council this morning. They're on their way now.' Fitzjohn looked at his watch. 'Or so I thought. If they take much longer, I won't have time to drop my suits off at my tailor before Reynolds and I speak to Stella Rossi.'

'I can wait here for the council to arrive, sir.'

Fitzjohn eyed Betts over his glasses. 'Have you ever had dealings with any councils, Betts?'

'No, but I've watched my mother in action. I'm sure I've learnt something along the way. If you like, I can get Mum over here. She'll soon sort this out.'

'Thanks, but I think we'll leave your mother out of this. I'd appreciate it though if you could wait here for the people from the council to arrive. I'm expecting they'll come prepared to take that branch down and when they start cutting, I'm afraid Rhonda will go spare. To put it politely, she's highly strung.'

'You mean she's neurotic, sir.'

'I didn't say that, Betts. But be warned. Rhonda Butler is a daunting adversary.'

'Leave her to me, sir.'

Fitzjohn left his tailor's shop that morning preoccupied with thoughts of how Betts was getting on with the council, and with Rhonda Butler. Was the threatening tree branch finally being cut down, or had Rhonda halted proceedings by chaining herself to the offending branch? With this last thought in mind, Fitzjohn took his mobile phone from his coat pocket and started to punch in Betts's number when his attention was drawn to two men walking ahead, in deep conversation. Fitzjohn slowed his pace when he realised who they were. Chief Superintendent Grieg and Ron Carling? Together? For what purpose? Fitzjohn's thoughts went back to his meeting with Grieg the previous day, and the knowledge Grieg had of Graeme Wyngard's complaint about his yacht being impounded. Did this mean that Ron Carling was the mole?

Confused as well as perturbed, Fitzjohn jumped into the first taxi at a rank along O'Connell Street and sat back stiffly as it took off into the traffic. His mind traversed through all the years he had known Ron Carling. A man he had always considered his friend. Not to mention one who had made it clear, right from their first days on the force, that he did not like Grieg and would never consider working with him. So, if that was the case, what were Ron and Grieg doing together now?

This last thought lingered with Fitzjohn as he and Reynolds started out for their interview with Stella Rossi. And it continued until Reynolds pulled up outside her Cammeray home where a set of garage doors, and a tall wrought iron gate, was all that gave any hint that a house lay beyond. 'Right, Reynolds,' said Fitzjohn, climbing out of the car. 'Let's see if Mrs Rossi's alibi gels with Prentice's, shall we?' Fitzjohn opened the gate and the two officers descended a set of stone steps into a small secluded garden. The front door to the residence lay down yet another set of steps. After pressing the doorbell, they waited before the door opened and an attractive woman in her late forties appeared. Tall and willowy, her dark hair swept up and held by an elaborate comb, she looked guardedly at the two men. 'Can I help you?'

'Mrs Stella Rossi?'

'Yes.'

'I'm Detective Chief Inspector Fitzjohn, and this is Detective Sergeant Reynolds. We're from the New South Wales Police Force. We'd like to speak to you in connection with your husband, Michael Rossi. May we come in?'

'Yes, of course. Actually I'm glad you've come to see me,' she said as she led the way along a wide hallway that ran the full depth of the house. 'I heard about Michael's death on the news on Saturday morning, but I haven't heard anything since.' She glanced at Fitzjohn. 'I'm still having difficulty believing what happened to him.' They emerged into a large living, dining area, its floor to ceiling glass bi-fold doors and windows revealing magnificent views over Long Bay. 'Have a seat, gentlemen.' Stella Rossi gestured to several couches, not unlike the ones at the victim's home in Rushcutters Bay. 'Can I get you both a refreshment?'

'That's very kind, Mrs Rossi, but we're fine, thank you,' replied Fitzjohn.

Stella Rossi nodded and sat on a couch, smoothing down the snug white slacks she wore. 'I take it you know that Michael and I were separated.'

'Yes, we are aware of that, Mrs Rossi,' answered Fitzjohn, looking around the room as he settled himself. 'Did you have much contact with your husband after the separation?'

'Not a lot, no, but we did keep in touch. Mostly by telephone.'

'And when was the last time you spoke to him?'

'As a matter of fact, it was the day he died. I telephoned Michael to see how he was.' Stella Rossi caught Fitzjohn's questioning look. 'He was a complex man, Chief Inspector. I worried about him. I had no idea it would be the last time we'd speak.' She looked away, her eyes blinking back tears. 'You know, I've been thinking that if I hadn't left Michael, this would never have happened.'

Fitzjohn waited before he continued, 'I know this is difficult, Mrs Rossi, but to your knowledge, did your husband have any enemies?'

'Enemies?' Stella grabbed a tissue from the box on the coffee table in front of her and dabbed her nose. 'I don't know. It's been over two years since Michael and I have lived together. The only person I know who didn't like Michael is Robert Nesbit. And who could blame him.' Stella shook her head. 'I take it you know about the reason, so I won't bore you with a repetition.'

'We know that your husband and Robert Nesbit were business partners and friends at one time,' Mrs Rossi, 'so it would be helpful to us if you could fill us in on what happened to change that.'

For the next few minutes, Fitzjohn and Reynolds listened to Stella Rossi's account of her estranged husband's love affair with Robert Nesbit's wife. 'It ruined Robert's marriage, of course, not to mention our own.' Stella glanced out to a yacht moored in the harbour at the end of the garden. 'The ideal home for a man who loved yachts and sailing wouldn't you say, Chief Inspector? And yet he threw it all away. Our actions can be so life changing. It's frightening. Still, I can't grumble. Michael and I had an amicable settlement that left us both financially secure. He insisted I have the house. It appeased his conscience, I suppose.'

'So I take it you don't expect to be a beneficiary of your husband's estate,' said Fitzjohn.

'I wouldn't expect to be, but as it turns out, I am. Michael didn't change his will after we separated. I know because he told me. Again, I think it appeased his conscience.'

Fitzjohn nodded. 'There's just one other question I have to ask, Mrs Rossi, and that is, where were you on Friday evening between the hours of eight and midnight?'

A look of indignation came to Stella Rossi's face. 'You're not suggesting...'

'I'm sure you can appreciate the importance of knowing where everyone, who knew your husband was at the time of his death, Mrs Rossi.'

'Well, since you put it that way. I attended a function at the art gallery with my friend, Janet Gibson. You can check with her. We left the gallery around 8:30pm and then... I met another friend.' Stella hesitated. 'Actually, it's a rather delicate situation. You see, he's married.'

'Can you give us his name? So we can corroborate your alibi.'

Stella grimaced. 'Is that altogether necessary, Chief Inspector?'

'It is I'm afraid.'

'Well, this is embarrassing because I was with Nigel Prentice, Michael's business partner. We've been seeing each other for the last couple of months.' Stella Rossi caught Fitzjohn's eye. 'It's shabby of me I know, but I've been so lonely.'

'Might I ask how you and Nigel Prentice spent the evening, Mrs Rossi?'

'We went for a drive. Up as far as Colloroy, I think.'

'Well, their alibi's match, sir,' said Reynolds as he followed Fitzjohn back through the garden to the car. 'And you can't help but feel sorry for the poor woman, can you? She seems to think that if she hadn't left her husband, he might still be alive.'

'It's part of the human condition, Reynolds. We feel responsible and guilt for much of which we're not.' Fitzjohn climbed into the car and pulled his seat belt on, his thoughts going to Edith. 'Even so, let's not forget the fact that with the death of Michael Rossi, Stella Rossi and Nigel Prentice now own Rossi & Prentice Yachting Electronics Pty Ltd. Which means, they both had motive to kill our victim.'

An hour later Fitzjohn sat at his desk in the Incident Room at Kings Cross Police Station turning his pen end for end, his thoughts not only on whether Ron Carling was Chief Superintendent Grieg's mole, but also the fate of the tree branch. As he sat there lost in thought, the door opened and Betts walked in. Fitzjohn sat forward. 'Tell me that the branch has been taken down,' he said.

Betts shook his head and slumped into his chair. 'I'm sorry, sir. You were right. Rhonda Butler is one difficult woman. She threatened to phone the police if we touched the tree.'

'But you *are* the police, Betts.'

'That fact didn't sink in, sir.'

Fitzjohn threw his pen on to his desk. 'What did the people from the council suggest I do?'

'Unfortunately, Mrs Butler put the wind up them, sir, and they left in a hurry.'

'Mmm. Let me guess. Rhonda dropped a few names and told them that if they so much as looked at her tree, none of them would have jobs by tomorrow morning.' Betts nodded. 'It's her usual line of defence.'

'Well, it worked,' said Betts. 'They packed up and left. Said they be in touch.'

Fitzjohn nodded. 'Well, you did your best under the circumstances. Rhonda is an indomitable character. How did you get on with the insurance company?'

'I had better luck there, sir. As the solicitor said on Sunday, the beneficiary of Claudia Rossi's life insurance policy was her partner, Richard Edwards. The insurance company paid out the policy of one million dollars, but not until April of 2011. Almost a year after her death.'

'Has the Coroner's report on Claudia Rossi come through yet?' asked Fitzjohn.

'Yes, sir. It just arrived.' Betts took the report out of his briefcase and laid it on the desk in front of him. 'She died from hepatic failure. In layman's terms, acute liver failure. The postmortem examination revealed she'd ingested some form of fungi. And from her initial presentation at the hospital, it was thought to have been amanita phalloides. Otherwise known as death cap mushrooms.' Betts grimaced. 'It's a grisly death, sir.'

'It sounds it. Where are these mushrooms found?'

Betts turned to the next page. 'It says here they're originally from the northern hemisphere, but can be found in south-eastern Australia, predominantly in the suburbs of Adelaide, Canberra and Melbourne as well as some Victorian towns.'

'But not here in New South Wales?'

'No, sir.'

'So where did Claudia Rossi come by them, I wonder?'

'The Coroner's findings are inconclusive on that,' replied Betts, 'although it was thought she probably picked the mushrooms herself while she was on a visit to the National Art Gallery in Canberra. Apparently, Claudia travelled by car to Canberra in July, 2010 to do some work at the national gallery. I'm waiting for the gallery to confirm the exact dates she was there.' Betts handed the report to Fitzjohn.

For the next few minutes, Fitzjohn read through it. 'You're right, Betts,' he said at last. 'Dying by ingesting death cap mushrooms is a most grisly death. The poor woman.' He closed the report and sat back in his chair. 'That explains why the insurance company took their time paying out the policy. One million dollars is a tidy sum.'

'Both Claudia Rossi and Richard Edwards were life insured for the same amount, sir. Apparently a precaution so their mortgage could be paid out if something was to happen to either one of them.'

'Seems reasonable. But in light of the fact that Michael Rossi wanted to speak to his solicitor about the policy, I think we should spend some time finding out everything we can about Claudia Rossi, including the circumstances surrounding her death. And I think her partner, Richard Edwards, would be a good place to start.' As Fitzjohn spoke, the Incident Room door opened and Detective Senior Constable Williams walked in.

'I have that information you wanted on Robert Nesbit, sir,' he said.

'Ah, good. Take a seat, Williams,' said Fitzjohn, wondering again whether Williams or Ron Carling could be Grieg's mole. 'What do you have for us?'

Williams sauntered across the room to sit on the edge of a desk in front of Fitzjohn. 'Robert Nesbit is a naval architect, and was joint owner of a yacht design business until its collapse in December 2009. His partners were a Richard Edwards and the victim, Michael Rossi.'

'Richard Edwards?' Fitzjohn shot a look at Betts. 'Go on, Williams.'

'The collapse of the company happened not long after Michael Rossi pulled out of the business, taking his capital with him. Since then Mr Nesbit's life has changed dramatically. His marriage ended around the same time as the business. A number of his properties were sold off during the divorce settlement and he now lives in a modest apartment in Double Bay. He's still a member of the Cruising Yacht Club. A life member, actually. And well known in yachting circles. Apparently he can be found there most days.'

'And, it would seem, had motive to kill Michael Rossi,' added Fitzjohn. 'I think we'll have a word with Mr Nesbit.'

After arriving at the Cruising Yacht Club, Fitzjohn and Betts gained entrance and made their way through to a sun drenched deck overlooking the clubs marina, and Rushcutters Bay.

'Good afternoon, gentlemen.' Fitzjohn turned to see the barman looking expectantly at them. 'Can I get you something?' he asked as he wiped the counter.

'We're looking for Mr Robert Nesbit,' replied Fitzjohn. 'The attendant at the front desk said we'd find him out here.'

The barman nodded. 'He's the gentleman over there, sitting alone, wearing the blue shirt.'

'Thank you.' Followed by Betts, Fitzjohn made his way between the tables that buzzed with the lunchtime crowd. Robert Nesbit looked round as they approached. A commanding looking man in his late fifties with piercing blue eyes and a ruddy complexion, he gave them a questioning look.

'Mr Nesbit?' asked Fitzjohn.

'Yes.' Nesbit got to his feet. 'Can I help you?'

'We're from the New South Wales Police, Mr Nesbit. I'm Detective Chief Inspector Fitzjohn. This is Detective Sergeant Betts. We'd like to speak to you in connection with the death of Michael Rossi. Is there somewhere we can talk?'

'We can talk here, Chief Inspector.' Nesbit gestured to the other chairs at his table. 'As a matter of fact, I was just sitting here thinking about Mike. It's been an awful shock.'

'We understand you spoke to Nigel Prentice on Friday wishing to speak to Michael Rossi,' said Fitzjohn, settling himself into a chair opposite Nesbit.

'I did, but I was told that Mike was out of town and unavailable. I got him later on his mobile though.'

'I see. Was there any particular reason you wanted to speak to him?'

'Yes, it was about a mutual colleague, Richard Edwards. Richard's in St Vincent's Hospital, I'm afraid. He's very ill. He's not expected to live. I wanted to tell Mike how grave his condition has become, and also to pass on a message from Richard.'

'What was that message?'

'That Richard needed to speak to Mike about his sister, Claudia. I don't know what about. Richard didn't say.' Nesbit paused.

'Perhaps I should explain who Richard is, Chief Inspector. He was Claudia's partner. She died in 2010. The three of us, Mike, Richard and I had been in business together at one time.' Nesbit looked at his watch. 'I'm afraid that you're going to have to excuse me, gentlemen. I've got to get back to hospital. Is there anything else?'

'Just one thing,' said Fitzjohn. 'We understand you spoke to Michael Rossi, here at the club, on Friday night.'

'You're well informed, Chief Inspector. Yes, we did speak on Friday night, after Mike had been to the hospital.'

'Did he say why Richard Edwards had wanted to speak to him?'

'No. He just told me that Richard wasn't expected to make it through the night.'

'Do you know what time Michael Rossi left the club?'

'It was just before 8pm. I remember because I left a few minutes later.'

'And where were you going, Mr Nesbit?'

'Back to the hospital.'

'I see. How long were you there?'

'Until quite late. Eleven or so.'

'And Mr Edwards never made any indication as to what he spoke to Michael Rossi about?'

'No. He wasn't conscious for most of the time I was there.'

'When you left the CYC on Friday evening, did you see anyone about?'

'There were a few people out walking. It was a warm night.' Robert Nesbit flinched as his mobile rang. 'Excuse me.' Nesbit answered the call and his face darkened before he said, 'Richard died a few minutes ago.'

Fitzjohn and Betts emerged from the CYC and made their way back to their car. 'Well, it seems it was Richard Edwards and something concerning Claudia that prompted Michael Rossi to return to Sydney early last Friday, Betts. Now we just have to find out what it was all about.' Fitzjohn sat back in the passenger seat of the car as Betts turned the ignition. 'It's unfortunate we weren't able to speak to Richard Edwards, but it wasn't to be. Whatever he spoke to our victim about died with him.' Fitzjohn paused. 'Let's turn our attention to Robert Nesbit. Make some enquiries, Betts. I want confirmation that he was at St Vincent's Hospital for the entire evening on Friday.'

'Yes, sir.'

{CHAPTER 13}

Next morning, Fitzjohn arrived at Kings Cross Police Station at first light, a routine he had followed since Edith's death. After tending his beloved orchids, he rarely lingered at home where his thoughts might dwell on the past. Instead, he found the early hour an ideal time to ponder his investigations before the day got underway. But this morning when he opened the Incident Room door, he was not alone.

Ron Carling, bent over Fitzjohn's desk, straightened when the door opened. 'Ah, Alistair. Just looking for some papers. I thought I might have left them here after our meeting last night. Seems I didn't.'

Carling gave a quick smile as Fitzjohn's thoughts went back to the previous day when he had chanced to see Ron talking to Chief Superintendent Grieg. The possibility that Ron could be Grieg's mole filled Fitzjohn with not only disappointment, but a certain sense of loss. After all, he and Ron were part of that dwindling, older establishment of detectives. They went back a long way, and even though they had rarely worked together, a certain amount of trust had built up as their paths crossed over the years. Or so Fitzjohn thought. Had he been wrong?

Placing his briefcase on the desk Fitzjohn removed his suit coat and hung it on the back of the chair as he tried to think of a way to find out whether his suspicions about Ron were correct. 'I'll let you know if they turn up,' he said, sitting down as Ron turned to leave. 'By the way,' he continued, 'I want to thank you for all your help getting Betts and me settled in. And for the investigative team you've provided. They're excellent. Thank you.'

'We aim to please,' said Ron, smiling. 'How's the investigation going anyway?'

'It's coming along. And as you said on my arrival. My secondment has its advantages in that it's a respite from Grieg, although having said that, he still manages to make his presence felt.'

'Oh? In what way?' Ron sat down on the corner of one of the desks.

'Grieg's got a mole,' said Fitzjohn.

'A mole? Here?' Carling chuckled. 'You're becoming paranoid, Alistair.'

'I wish I was.'

'What on earth makes you think that?' asked Ron Carling.

'Because yesterday when I spoke to Grieg, he knew things about my investigation that he couldn't possibly know. Not without an informant.'

'Do you have any thoughts on who it might be?'

At that moment, the Incident Room door opened and Betts walked in. Ron Carling jumped off the desk.

'Well, I'd better get a move on. We can continue this conversation later.' Ron acknowledged Betts as he left the room.

'Any word on Whitehead, Betts?' asked Fitzjohn opening his briefcase and taking his papers out.

'Yes, sir. It seems the real Pierce Whitehead died three years ago in a light plane crash in South Africa.' The papers Fitzjohn held fell on to the desk. 'Isn't that around the same time our winemaker friend was employed by Claudia Rossi to manage Five Oaks Winery?'

'Yes, sir. Charlotte Rossi said her mother hired Whitehead in 2010 on a five year contract.' Betts sat down at his desk. 'I've got a couple of the guys looking into who our Pierce Whitehead really is.'

'Good,' said Fitzjohn. 'Hopefully it doesn't take too long. However, in the meantime, I think it best we keep referring to him as Pierce Whitehead. Just to prevent any confusion. And I want him watched in case he gets the idea that we're on to him.'

'Now, I'd like to go through everything once again, Betts, but before we start, there's something I want to ask you.'

'What's that, sir?'

Fitzjohn hesitated before deciding not to tell Betts about the suspected mole. 'On second thought, it can wait.' Fitzjohn reorganised the papers on his desk. 'What do we have?'

Betts looked back down at his notes, tapping his pen on the desk before he said, 'The way I see it, we've got two people who benefit financially from Michael Rossi's death. His niece, Charlotte Rossi, and his estranged wife, Stella Rossi. The imposter, Whitehead, and Nesbit only had their pride and anger to satisfy.'

'And what about Prentice?' asked Fitzjohn removing his glasses, and placing them carefully on to his desk.'

'Well, if Prentice did get word that Michael Rossi planned to buy him out of the business, not only did he have the motive to kill Rossi, but I daresay the opportunity as well as the means, sir.'

'True,' replied Fitzjohn, putting his glasses back on, and looking around at the whiteboard. 'What about Robert Nesbit? Any joy from the staff at the hospital?'

Betts turned the page of his notebook. 'I spoke to the nurse who was on duty on Friday night. She remembered Richard Edwards having two visitors. The first, a man answering the victim's description. He arrived around 3:20pm just as she started her shift, and left about 40 minutes later. A second man, identifying himself as Robert Nesbit, arrived about 8:30pm.'

'Did she notice what time Nesbit left?'

'No, sir.'

Fitzjohn leaned back in his chair. 'So, Nesbit could have left the hospital at anytime during that evening. Gone back to Rushcutters Bay, killed the victim and returned to the hospital. Have another word with the staff on duty that night, Betts. See if anyone noticed Robert Nesbit coming or going.'

Fitzjohn got to his feet and commenced pacing the length of the Incident Room. 'Let's turn our attention to our victim, Michael Rossi. You say he left the hospital just after 4pm. Yet he didn't arrive at Esme Timmons's home until six that evening. So, where was he in those intervening two hours?'

'Presumably trying, and not finding whatever he was looking for, later, in his sister's study, sir,' answered Betts. 'Speaking of which. Charlotte Rossi called into the station today to report that Miss Timmons has found something missing from the study, after all.' Betts looked down at his notebook again. 'It's described as a Limoges, porcelain footed perfume bottle. Hand painted in violets on a cream background. Oh and there's a small nick in one of its feet. The makers mark is D & Co France.' Betts looked up. 'Shouldn't be too difficult to identify if it turns up.'

'Did Ms Rossi know its value?' asked Fitzjohn.

'No, sir. She just said it has a great deal of sentimental value for Miss Timmons. It's a family heirloom.' Betts leaned back in his chair. 'It could mean that the break-in had nothing to do with Michael Rossi's death, sir. Or, the perfume bottle was taken to make us think that. Especially in light of the forensic report I've just received concerning Claudia Rossi's diary.' Betts handed the report to Fitzjohn and the continued. 'The report concludes that the slip of paper found in the victim's hand, did come from Claudia Rossi's diary.'

'Did forensics find anything written on that piece of paper,' asked Fitzjohn.

'No, sir.'

Fitzjohn looked thoughtful. 'Well, even though Michael Rossi took the diary with him when he left Esme Timmons's home on Friday evening, it doesn't mean to say it was a significant factor in his death. But having said that, I want a list of everyone mentioned in that diary.'

'It's done, sir.' Betts grinned, handing Fitzjohn the list. 'Among them are Claudia Rossi's friend, Phillipa Braithwaite, and two men. Aiden Maxwell and a Douglas Porteous. Maxwell's an art dealer. He has three commercial galleries. Two here in Sydney, in Paddington and Mosman, and a third in Carlton in Melbourne. As it happens, Phillipa Braithwaite manages the Mosman gallery as well as the one in Melbourne.'

'We met Phillipa Braithwaite when we first spoke to Charlotte Rossi, didn't we? A friend of Claudia's since school days, I seem to remember Miss Timmons saying.'

'Yes, sir.'

'And Douglas Porteous? Who is he, exactly?'

'I have Williams working on that, sir.'

'Then let's start with Phillipa Braithwaite. Being an old school friend, she might be able to help us piece together Claudia Rossi's movements in the time leading up to her death. Where can we find her, Betts?'

'At the Mosman gallery, sir.'

———

After crossing the Harbour Bridge to the North Shore, Betts tapped his fingers impatiently on the steering wheel as they continued, at a snail's pace, along Military Road.

'Where exactly is this gallery?' asked Fitzjohn.

'Cowles Road, sir. At this next set of lights.' Betts did a quick right turn into a tree-lined street, awash with cafes and boutiques. He pulled over to the curb in front of a gallery nestled amongst them. 'This is it, sir.'

'The ArtSpace Gallery,' said Fitzjohn, peering out of the passenger window. 'Looks impressive, but I think we may have come at a bad time.' Betts followed Fitzjohn's gaze to see a short, dark haired man carrying two large bouquets of white carnations. Muttering to himself, he headed for a white van. Behind him came a tall, shapely woman wearing a colourful, blousy, top over a pair of slim line slacks.

'That's her, isn't it, Betts?' asked Fitzjohn. 'Phillipa Braithwaite?'

'Yes, sir.'

Fitzjohn and Betts left their car.

'You do understand, don't you, Mr Mason? I did specifically order red roses.' With her claims ignored, Phillipa threw her hands in the air and turned back. As she did so, she caught sight of Fitzjohn and Betts at the curb.

'Looks like we've caught you at a bad time, Ms Braithwaite,' said Fitzjohn.

With a puzzled look, Phillipa stared at Fitzjohn before a smile came to her face. 'It's Chief Inspector Fitzjohn, isn't it? You brought the awful news to Charlotte about Michael Rossi last Saturday morning.'

'Yes. And this is Detective Sergeant Betts.'

'Of course.' Phillipa pushed her long wavy brown hair back from her face, her dark eyes flashing. 'You'll have to excuse all the fuss. We're in the throes of preparing for an exhibition this afternoon.' She glanced disapprovingly at the florist's van, pulling away from the curb. 'Not everything is going to plan.' Phillipa hesitated. 'Is there something I can do for you, Chief Inspector?'

'We wondered whether you could answer a few questions, Ms Braithwaite; concerning Claudia Rossi.'

'Claudia?' Phillipa Braithwaite's brow furrowed. 'Well, yes, of course. Come inside, won't you.'

Fitzjohn and Betts followed Phillipa into the gallery.

'I see you showcase a wide variety of work,' said Fitzjohn, looking around.

'We do,' replied Phillipa, appearing pleased at Fitzjohn's interest. 'And it's been a huge success. At different times, you can find not only paintings in various mediums, but sculpture, photography and ceramics. But as you can see, at the moment, it's all a bit of a mess. I think we'll talk in my office.' Fitzjohn and Betts followed Phillipa through the maze of people and paintings to a windowless room at the back of the gallery. 'It's not ideal, but I guarantee it will be quiet,' she said closing the door. 'Won't you sit down?' Fitzjohn and Betts settled themselves, Betts fumbling for his notebook. Phillipa sat in a large swivel chair, clasping her hands together on the desk. 'Now, you said you wanted to ask me about Claudia.'

'Yes,' replied Fitzjohn. 'We understand you two were friends.'

'We were.' Phillipa smiled to herself. 'We became friends on our first day at boarding school, here in Sydney. We were both twelve at the time. Claudia's parents had decided it was to her benefit to be educated in the city, and mine... well, mine were in the midst of a rather nasty divorce.' Phillipa paused. 'What exactly do you want to know, Chief Inspector?'

'We're trying to piece together Claudia's movements just prior to her death.'

'Oh.' Phillipa gave Fitzjohn a quizzical look. 'Well, it was quite some time ago.'

'So we understand,' said Fitzjohn. 'The week of July 11th, 2010, to be exact.'

'So it was. Well, Claudia and I had planned to have dinner together on the Thursday evening of that week, but she cancelled at the last minute. She said her brother, Michael, had asked her to make up numbers at his dinner party. So as it turned out, I didn't see her at all before she became ill. We only spoke on the telephone. And that was when she rang to cancel our dinner engagement.'

'Did she speak about anything else when she rang, Ms Braithwaite?' asked Fitzjohn.

Phillipa thought for a moment. 'She did, as a matter of fact. You know, after all that's happened, I'd almost forgotten about it. She told me she'd just had another row with Richard. He was her partner. They'd separated earlier in 2010, and had just got back together again. She was upset because she suspected that Richard was straying again. She said she thought she'd made a mistake to take him back. It was the last conversation we had.' Phillipa fell silent as if reflecting on that conversation.

'We understand she died from liver failure caused by ingesting a particular lethal type of mushroom,' continued Fitzjohn, taking the conversation on to a different path. 'A mushroom that isn't found here in New South Wales. It is, however, found in Canberra, and we understand that Claudia spent some time there before she died. Do you know if Claudia was in a habit of picking wild mushrooms, Ms Braithwaite?'

'She did if she came across them when she was out walking in the mornings. I know because she'd done so when we'd walked together. But as you say, the variety that killed her doesn't grow here in New South Wales. At the inquest, it was thought she'd picked them while she'd been in Canberra during that week. But you probably know that already.' Phillipa paused. 'Can I ask why you're enquiring about Claudia, Chief Inspector? I thought you were investigating Michael's death?'

'We are, Ms Braithwaite, but in so doing, questions about his sister' death have been raised.'

'Well, all that I can tell you is that Claudia and Michael were very close. He was devastated when she died. They were twins, of course, so perhaps the tie is greater. I don't know.' Phillipa sighed.

'When was the last time you saw Michael Rossi, Ms Braithwaite?'

'Oh. I can't remember exactly. And the only place we ever did meet up was if he happened to drop in to see Charlotte when I was there.'

'So presumably, not someone you knew well.'

'No.'

'Very well. I think that will be all then,' said Fitzjohn, getting to his feet. 'Oh. There is something else. I understand you manage this gallery for a man by the name of Aiden Maxwell.'

'Yes. I have done since it opened in 2008.'

'Right. It's just that Claudia had Mr Maxwell's name penciled into her diary. Can you tell us what connection she had with him?'

'It was restoration work. Aiden used Claudia's expertise in that area on many occasions. And she's sadly missed, I might add.'

Fitzjohn and Betts made their way, once again, through the commotion in the gallery, and out to their car. 'Well, Betts. We didn't learn much more about Claudia Rossi other than she cancelled having dinner with Phillipa Braithwaite two days before she died.' Fitzjohn sighed and pulled his seat belt on. 'I want you to pay a call to the New South Wales Art Gallery next, where Claudia used to work. You never know, Michael Rossi might have called in there on Friday if he was making enquiries about his sister. Oh, and have a word to Charlotte Rossi about her mother too. While you're doing that, I'll speak to that art dealer, Aiden Maxwell.'

Fitzjohn arrived at the Paddington gallery amidst an exhibition. Undaunted, if not pleased, he made his way unobtrusively inside, welcoming the opportunity to view each painting he passed. 'Welcome to our exhibition, sir,' said a voice all too soon. Fitzjohn turned to see a young fair-haired man with a wide smile. 'This is our program,' he continued, handing Fitzjohn a colourful brochure. 'If there's anything I can help you with, please don't hesitate to ask.'

'There is as a matter of fact,' said Fitzjohn, taking the brochure. 'I'm here to see Aiden Maxwell.' The young man smiled.

'Ah. Our exalted leader. Now, where did I see him last,' he said, looking around the crowded space. 'Yes, there he is on the mezzanine level, sir. The fellow in the dark blue suit and red bow tie.' As he spoke, the man with the bow tie looked down over the railing. 'This gentleman would like to speak to you Aiden.'

Fitzjohn made his way through the gathering to the foot of a spiral staircase to be met by Maxwell as he descended. A slim man with fine sharp features, Fitzjohn detected an air of smoothness about him. 'Is there a particular piece you're interested in, Mr...?'

'It's Detective Chief Inspector Fitzjohn. I'm from the New South Wales Police.' Fitzjohn noted Maxwell's disapproving air. 'I realise this isn't the most appropriate time...'

'You're right, it isn't.' Maxwell's eyes narrowed.

'Nevertheless,' said Fitzjohn, undaunted. 'Is there somewhere we can talk?'

Maxwell pursed his lips. 'Follow me, *Chief* Inspector.'

Fitzjohn fell into step with Maxwell. 'It's a fine exhibition. I regret my visit doesn't allow me the time to enjoy it.' Maxwell passed Fitzjohn a churlish look as he opened the door to his office. Lavish beyond his expectations, Fitzjohn took in the exquisite detail on the Chippendale desk with its inlay and marquetry of flowers and birds. A piece of art in itself, he thought.

The paintings on the walls and tufted leather chairs added to the richness of the room.

'Have a seat, Chief Inspector.' Maxwell settled himself behind his desk, sitting back and eyeing Fitzjohn with an air of arrogance. 'Now, what can I do for you?'

Fitzjohn sank into one of the leather chairs in front of the desk, delighting in its comfort and, at the same time, aware of Maxwell's distain. 'I'm investigating the death of a man by the name of Michael Rossi, Mr Maxwell, and my inquiries have led me to you.' Fitzjohn met Maxwell's intense gaze. 'Primarily because I understand you knew the victim's sister, Claudia Rossi.'

'Claudia? Yes, I did know her. She did restoration work for me. She died some time ago.'

'Speaking of which. When did you last see Claudia Rossi, Mr Maxwell?'

'Oh.' Maxwell's brow wrinkled. 'I'm not exactly sure of the date, but I know it was shortly before she died. That was in July 2010.'

'July 17th, 2010, to be exact. A Saturday,' said Fitzjohn.

'You're well informed, Chief Inspector. And that makes it easy for me because I know Claudia came to see me the Sunday before she died. So, the last time I saw her would have been July 11th. As I remember, she wanted to ask about the provenance of a piece of art that the New South Wales Gallery had purchased. She worked for the Gallery. But I suppose you know that too.'

Ignoring Maxwell's last remark Fitzjohn continued. 'The matter must have been urgent for you to open the gallery specifically for her.'

'Well, at the time, Claudia seemed to think so, but as it turned out, it was a minor misunderstanding in that she had contacted the wrong person about the provenance.'

'How long did your meeting last?'

'About forty-five minutes as I remember. What exactly are you trying to find out, Chief Inspector?'

'Who killed her, Mr Maxwell?'

Maxwell's chair brought him forward with a jolt, his face contorted. 'I don't understand. I thought Claudia died of liver failure.'

Fitzjohn returned to Kings Cross Police Station somewhat annoyed, Maxwell's pompous demeanor having exhausted his patience. He found Betts in the Incident Room sitting back with his legs on his desk. 'I'm glad you have time to relax, Detective Sergeant,' he said as he walked into the room. Betts's feet hit the floor with a thud.

'How did you get on with Charlotte Rossi?'

'I didn't, sir. That is. According to her shop assistant, she's away until Thursday. She and Esme Timmons have gone to the winery. I had a bit more luck at the New South Wales Art Gallery though. Someone remembered Michael Rossi asking to speak to Marian Davies. Apparently, she and Claudia used to work together.'

'And…?'

'It's a 'but', sir. Ms Davies is attending a funeral in rural New South Wales. She's expected back in Sydney tomorrow.'

Fitzjohn sighed. 'Right. Then I want to see her as soon as she gets back. Let's hope Michael Rossi did seek her out. I also want to ask her if she knows anything about Claudia Rossi's dealings with Aiden Maxwell.'

'How did it go with Aiden Maxwell?' asked Betts.

'He confirmed that Claudia did restoration work for him, and that he had a meeting with her a week before she died. Apparently, it was to do with a painting that the New South Wales Art Gallery had purchased. Marian Davies will probably know about it seeing that she and Claudia Rossi were colleagues.'

{CHAPTER 14}

The unique smell peculiar to old bookshops and libraries permeated the air as Charlotte opened the door on Monday morning. She had hoped for a few minutes to herself before her assistant, Irene Forbes, arrived, but it was not to be. Irene, her thick frame balanced precariously on a stepladder, was already busy flicking a red duster along the spines of the books on one of the top shelves, while humming to herself. When the little gold bell on the back of the bookshop door sounded, she turned suddenly. A diligent and trustworthy assistant, yes; Charlotte knew she was lucky to have Irene, but today she suspected that Irene's incessant gushiness would grate on her nerves.

'Charlotte. You poor thing,' she said climbing down, her feet hitting the floor with a clump. 'I heard about your Uncle Michael over the weekend, and I'm *so* sorry.' Irene scurried across the room. 'I didn't expect you to come in today. Are you sure you're feeling up to it?'

'Actually, I won't be here for long,' said Charlotte, moving passed Irene to the desk at the back corner of the bookshop. 'I'm driving up to Five Oaks and taking Esme with me. This whole affair has been difficult for her.' Charlotte sat down not wanting to elaborate. Instead, she watched the red duster move along the edge of the desk, and waited for Irene's inquisitive nature to move into gear.

'I'm sure it has. Esme must be devastated. I suppose it's too early for the police to know who did it.'

Charlotte met Irene's look of anticipation. 'Yes, it's far too early to know anything.' Charlotte sifted through the mail on the desk, hoping to dissuade her assistant from asking any further questions. She tossed the usual advertising material aside until she came to a long narrow envelope and a smaller one, both from 'Spencer, Anderson & Sumner, Solicitors.' Irene's duster came to an abrupt halt.

'Those two envelopes were delivered by courier just after I arrived this morning,' she offered. 'The long one is the type used for wills. I know because I once worked in a solicitor's office. Did I ever tell you about that?'

'No, you didn't.' Charlotte put the envelopes aside and got to her feet, aware her annoyance was beginning to show. 'I think I'll make a cup of coffee. Would you like one, Irene?'

Irene's gaze shifted from the envelopes to Charlotte. 'Yes, in fact, why don't I make it? You carry on here.'

Charlotte waited until Irene disappeared into the small kitchen at the rear of the bookshop before she picked up the smaller of the two envelopes, tore it open and read its contents.

"Dear Ms Rossi,

This is to advise that you have been named in Michael Rossi's Last Will and Testament as the beneficiary of his fifty percent share in Five Oaks Winery. A copy of Mr Rossi's will has been sent under separate cover for your perusal.

Please contact my office at your earliest convenience for further details in this matter.

Yours sincerely

David W. Spencer
Principal,
Spencer Anderson Sumner, Solicitors"

Charlotte sat back feeling a mixture of relief as well as sadness. Relief because Michael had left his shares in the winery to her, and sadness in the way she had come by them. As these thoughts ran through her mind, Irene reappeared with two steaming mugs of coffee.

'I hope it wasn't bad news,' she said, putting the two mugs on the desk before pulling up the nearest chair.

'No, it wasn't.' As Irene sat down, Charlotte realised she was about to face a barrage of questions. 'Oh. I didn't realise the time,' she said, looking at her watch. 'We'd better open up.' Reluctantly, Irene bustled away, and Charlotte slid the letter from the solicitor, and the large envelope containing the will, into her handbag. When she looked back up, Pierce Whitehead was standing in front of her desk.

'Pierce.'

'Hello, Charlotte. I heard about Michael and I came by to offer both my condolences, and my support. Is there anything I can do?' he asked, pulling up a chair.

Charlotte tensed as she usually did when faced with Pierce Whitehead's unpleasant suave. 'Thanks, but there isn't.'

'Well then, I want you to promise me that if you need anything, anything at all, you'll let me know. And I want to assure you I don't know anything about Michael's death.'

Charlotte's hand knocked her mug of coffee sending droplets over its edge. She grabbed a tissue to soak them up and glared at Pierce. 'The thought never entered my mind,' she replied.

'Even so, I felt I should say something because as you can appreciate, with Michael firing me after that row we had in the middle of the harvest, it could be construed…'

'Michael *fired* you?'

'Don't tell me you didn't know.' Charlotte's skin tingled as Pierce's mood changed to one of indignation. 'I suppose he told you I *quit*.'

Charlotte bristled. 'Yes, as a matter of fact, he did.'

Pierce sat back holding up his hands. 'Look, I'm sorry. I'm not angry with you. It's just that my whole life has been turned upside down. Same for you, I guess, with what's happened to Michael.' When Charlotte did not reply, Pierce continued. 'Are you still planning on selling Five Oaks? It's just that if you don't sell, I feel compelled to mention that…'

'What?'

'It's just a word of warning that's all. About Rafe Simms.'

'Rafe? What about him?'

'I don't know if you're aware,' said Pierce, 'but Rafe Simms has coveted Five Oaks for years as did his father before him.'

Charlotte frowned. 'Is that what my mother told you?'

'Not in so many words, no, but she did make it clear that she didn't like Rafe Simms or his family.'

'I'm aware of that,' said Charlotte, 'but I don't think it had anything to do with the winery.' Charlotte threw the coffee soaked tissue into the wastepaper bin. At the same time, she noticed the growing number of people now browsing the shelves of the bookshop. 'Will you excuse me for a minute, Pierce, while I attend to my customers?'

'Yes, of course. In fact, I've got to go anyway.' Pierce jumped to his feet. 'But before I do, I want to thank you for standing as my referee for the winery position. I do appreciate it.'

'Don't mention it. I'm happy to oblige,' replied Charlotte.

Relieved as the door closed behind Pierce Whitehead, Charlotte turned and smiled at a woman approaching with a book in her hand. 'Good morning, madam. Sorry to keep you waiting.' A number of thoughts raced through Charlotte's mind as she served her customer, not the least of which was her impending visit to Five Oaks, and seeing Rafe Simms again.

Esme, dressed in a pair of white slacks and a pale pink blouse, settled herself into the passenger seat of Charlotte's car as they set off for the Hunter Valley and Five Oaks Winery. 'I'm really looking forward to seeing the place again,' said Esme. 'The last time I was there was when we had that surprise party for your mother's fiftieth birthday.' Esme fingered the pearl necklace she wore and looked out of the side window of the car as Charlotte maneuvered her way through the traffic on the Pacific Highway. 'Of course, when I was young, I spent quite a bit of time there. Especially during harvest time,' she continued. 'Your grandfather liked to get as much help as possible.' Esme sighed. 'They were such good times.'

'We'll have a lovely couple of days, Esme,' said Charlotte. 'It's just what we both need.'

'I'm sure it is, my dear.'

They fell into silence until they emerged from the city on to the open freeway and Esme surfaced from her thoughts of days gone by. 'Have you made a decision about whether you'll pursue the provenance of that sketch, Charlotte, because I've been thinking, having the provenance correct will be invaluable if you decide to sell.'

'I had decided not to bother Esme, but last night I found the name of a previous owner in that report. A man by the name of Douglas Porteous. I thought I'd contact him to get the name of the person he bought the sketch from.'

Passing through Cessnock they drove on until the car topped a small rise in the road, and there before them lay a patchwork of vineyards stretching as far as the eye could see. Esme took a breath. 'Oh, look at that. Such simple beauty.'

Charlotte slowed the car when they neared Five Oaks Winery, its entrance marked only by a small sign moving gently with the breeze. Turning into the property, they continued along the dirt road, the rows of vines on each side standing like sentinels to the family's years of wine growing. In the distance, the original river stone cottage with its various extensions came into view. Surrounded by lawns and giant trees, it appeared a cool oasis in the blazing sun. Charlotte pulled up at the base of the steps leading on to the wide verandah.

'It seems very quiet,' said Esme, getting out of the car. 'I thought it'd be a beehive of activity with the harvest in full swing.'

'So did I,' replied Charlotte, looking back over the vineyard. Perhaps they've finished.' Charlotte carried the bags on to the verandah where she set them down and opened the front door.

'Oh, it's good to come back,' said Esme as she walked into the front hall. 'This house always did have such a comfortable atmosphere.'

Charlotte set the bags down. 'I'll help you get settled, Esme.'

'You don't have to do that, dear. I know you're anxious to find out about the harvest so why don't you go along and do that. I'll be fine here. I'm going to have a look around, and then I'll make myself a cup of tea.'

'Well, if you're sure, Esme. I won't be long.'

With apprehension tinged with excitement, Charlotte stepped back outside and walked toward the building that housed the cool room where the grapes were stored. It was the first time she had been back to Five Oaks since that fateful day, eighteen months earlier when Richard Edwards had telephoned to say that her mother had been hospitalised with liver failure. The day her life changed forever. Rounding the side of the old building, she could see Rafe's battered green truck parked outside the main entrance. The door to the cool room stood ajar. Tentatively, Charlotte peeked inside to find his tall frame enveloped in a pair of jeans and a white shirt. He looked up when she appeared. 'Hello, Rafe.'

In his mid-thirties, Rafe's aquiline features froze. 'Charlotte.'

Charlotte could feel his unease. 'I'm sorry. I should have let you know I was coming.'

'No, not at all. You just took me by surprise, that's all. It's wonderful to see you,' he said haltingly. 'I'm sorry about Michael. I couldn't believe it when I heard.' As the words left his lips, another voice sounded from outside.

'Rafe. Are you in there? I'm returning your phone. You left it in my...' Charlotte turned to see a tall young woman with long auburn hair and almond shaped eyes. 'Oh, I'm sorry,' she said cheerily. 'I didn't realise we had company.'

'Sally, this is Charlotte Rossi,' said Rafe. 'Michael's niece.'

'Oh.' An awkward silence filled the room before Sally continued. 'Sally Webster, I'm pleased to meet you, Charlotte,' she said, holding out her hand. 'I'm sorry about your uncle. We both are. Aren't we, darling?' she said, looking up at Rafe as she moved to his side. 'If there's anything we can do...'

Charlotte tried to gather herself. 'That's kind of you, but I think everything that can be done is being done. We just have to wait to see what the police investigation reveals.'

'Yes, of course.' Sally paused. 'Actually I feel like I know you already.' With Charlotte's questioning look, Sally continued. 'I'm managing the wine tasting cellar for Rafe, but I've also been helping with the paperwork concerning your grape harvest. Speaking of which, I'm going to have to get back over to the office to finish it off,' she said, squeezing Rafe's forearm and handing him his phone. 'I hope to see you again while you're here, Charlotte.'

'I hope so too,' lied Charlotte, her initial elation at seeing Rafe quelled as she watched Sally's receding back. Why did she feel like this? After all, she was the one who had ended their relationship. Did she expect Rafe to be here, alone, waiting for her? A void of silence followed Sally's departure. 'I take it you've finished the harvest,' she said at last, in an attempt to fill that silence.

'Yes. As of late yesterday. I'll be depositing the agreed amount into Five Oaks Winery's bank account when Sally's completed the paperwork.' Another silence followed before Rafe said. 'Sally's on a working holiday from the UK. I hired her when I opened the wine tasting cellar at the beginning of the summer. She's helped me get it off the ground. She has experience in marketing...'

'It's okay, Rafe. You don't have to explain.' Charlotte bit her upper lip. 'Life goes on. I should have let you know I was driving up from Sydney.' Another awkward silence ensued, Charlotte's thoughts spinning out of control. Why had she come here unannounced?

'If there's anything I can do to help while you're here, Charlotte, you only have to ask. I know it's a difficult time.'

Taking the opportunity to change the direction of the conversation Charlotte replied, 'I did want to ask you about Michael. I thought you might know why he returned to Sydney on Friday. It was so unlike him to change his plans.'

'You're right, it was, but as I told the police, Michael didn't say why he was leaving early. He just said something had come up and he had to get back. We'd spent the morning together. I showed him the progress we'd made with the harvest and after lunch, I left him in the study at the house to look for the extra set of keys to the property, as well as the necessary papers regarding the winery before the real estate agent arrived. When I next saw him, oh, probably half an hour later, he said he was leaving.'

'I wonder what happened in that half hour,' Charlotte said as if to herself.

'I don't know, but he was speaking to someone on the phone when I went in to see him. And he looked fairly distressed. I told the police. I'm sure they'll find out who he spoke to when they check out his phone.'

Charlotte started toward the door. 'I'd better get back to the house. I brought Esme with me and I want to help her get settled.'

'How long are you staying?' asked Rafe as they emerged from the building.

'Just a couple of nights.'

'Are you planning on going ahead with the sale?' he asked. 'It's just that the real estate agent left me his card when he finally got here last Friday and I said I'd pass it on. I've got it here.' Rafe pulled out his wallet and gave Charlotte the card.

'Thanks.' Charlotte studied the card. 'I'll give him a ring. He needs to know that the property can't be listed until Michael's estate is finalised. Which is just as well because I'm not sure what I'm going to do yet. Selling Five Oaks was really Michael's idea not mine.' Charlotte gave a quick smile.

'Well, in making your decision just keep in mind how difficult it can be to run a winery from a distance when you have to rely on someone you've employed.' Rafe hesitated. 'I'm not trying to put you off or anything, Charlotte. 'It's just that… Well, I'm sure you'll come to the right decision.'

'I'm sure I shall,' she replied.

'I should ask then whether you'd like me to carry on for the time being. It's just that there's still quite a bit that needs to be done. I'm happy to continue with the arrangement I made with Michael.'

Charlotte felt Rafe's impersonal edge, and her thoughts went to Pierce Whitehead's warning that Rafe coveted Five Oaks Winery. Was it true?' She tried to dismiss the thought. She knew why her mother did not like Rafe Simms, and it was nothing to do with

Five Oaks. How can I be swayed by something Pierce Whitehead told me, she argued with herself. 'Yes. I'd appreciate that, Rafe.'

'Fine then,' he said, smiling. 'I'll speak to you before you leave. It'll be nice to see Esme again. It's been a long time.'

A feeling of loss swept over Charlotte as she watched Rafe climb into his truck and give a nonchalant wave before driving off. Charlotte turned and started to walk slowly back toward the house. They had once been so close and at ease with each other. Rafe's uncharacteristic distance had unnerved her. But what did I expect, she thought. Our relationship has been over for a long time. Or have I only just realised that fact. It's my own fault for turning up here out of the blue. I've embarrassed him. Unless, of course, Pierce Whitehead is to be believed. As she reached the verandah of the house, she looked out across the endless rows of vines. This place is certainly worth coveting. Inside, she found Esme sitting in the living room looking through an old photo album.

'Oh, there you are, Charlotte. Were you able to speak to Rafe about the harvest?'

'Yes. It's all finished.' Charlotte slumped down into a chair.

'What is it, dear? You look a bit down.' Esme removed her glasses and put them on the table next to her chair before she closed the album. 'Has seeing Rafe again upset you?'

'You're very perceptive, Esme.'

'Well, it's understandable, isn't it? You two were engaged to be married. It can't have been easy seeing him again.'

'No. It wasn't,' said Charlotte, thinking about Sally. 'But it's also something he said that made me wonder... I'm probably wrong, but it was almost as though he was advising me to sell Five Oaks.' Charlotte recounted her conversations with Rafe. 'What do you think, Esme?'

Esme sat in thought for a minute or two. 'Perhaps he was merely letting you know the possible pitfalls you could face if you decide to run the winery from a distance. Although having said that, I seem to remember he did make an offer for Five Oaks just before your mother took over its management.'

'I didn't know that,' replied Charlotte.

'Oh, it was long before you and Rafe started seeing each other. And it was only a verbal offer, you understand, when he found out your grandfather planned to sell. I think it spurred your mother into a decision. She'd been undecided for months about taking on the winery, and your grandfather got tired of waiting.' Esme paused. 'And as far as Pierce Whitehead's claims about Rafe are concerned, I'm sure Pierce wouldn't know your mother's real reason for disliking Rafe. She'd never have disclosed that to a member of her staff.'

'I know you're right, but I can't help wondering...'

'About what?' asked Esme. 'About whether that was the reason he asked you to marry him?'

'Yes.'

'Charlotte. Do you really think that Rafe Simms is that sort of person?' Esme sighed. 'To be quite frank, my dear, I don't see that there's a dilemma. You turned Rafe down so as far as I can see, the matter's closed. Unless, of course, you're still in love with him.'

'It's too late for that, Esme. Rafe's moved on.'

'Oh. I see. Another woman.'

Charlotte nodded.

Esme got to her feet. 'Didn't you mention that you wanted to gather together all the papers that relate to the winery while we're here? I think this is a good time to do that. Let's get busy, my girl.' Charlotte followed Esme out of the living room and into the study. 'Oh, I remember this room when your grandfather was alive,' said Esme, standing in the doorway. 'And it's almost as he left it.' Esme cast her eyes around before they came to rest on a photograph on the wall above the bureau. 'I remember when this was taken,' she said, walking over. 'It was just after I'd got news that Thomas was lost in action. Your grandmother, my sister, invited me here to stay with them for a while.' Esme fell silent before her gaze lowered to the bureau beneath the photograph. 'And this bureau was Thomas's. I gave it to your grandfather. He and Thomas had been good friends.' Esme opened the bureau letting down the writing desk. 'I seem to remember a hidden compartment here somewhere. I used to keep Thomas's letters in it. And if I'm not mistaken...' As Esme pushed the surface above the desktop, a small drawer popped open. 'Voila!' A smile of satisfaction came to Esme's face before it turned to one of surprise. 'Oh, look, there are still letters inside. Surely they're not mine.' Esme peered into the small space and her smile faded.

'What is it?' asked Charlotte.

'There are three letters here. All addressed to your mother.' Esme handed the envelopes to Charlotte.

Charlotte studied each one. 'Should we open them? Or should we put them back.' She looked across at Esme. 'After all, letters are private. Even when you've passed away.'

'It's up to you, Charlotte.'

'Well, the addresses on the envelopes are printed so I doubt they're personal. I'll just have a peak,' she said with a smile. Charlotte took the first letter from its envelope, unfolded it and gasped.

'What is it?'

Charlotte handed the letter to Esme. 'It's not a proper letter, Esme. The words have been pieced together from newspaper and magazine print. And look what it says. It reads like a poison pen letter. Who would send such letters?'

Esme put her glasses on and read the letter. 'Someone with a twisted mind,' she said, frowning.

❦ CHAPTER 15 ❧

C harlotte sat at one of the coffee shop's outdoor tables, absentmindedly turning the pages of the morning paper. The letters she and Esme had found at the winery the day before played on her mind, overshadowing her thoughts about Michael's death.

'You're back.' Charlotte looked up to see Phillipa Braithwaite. 'I called at the bookshop yesterday and Irene said you and Esme had gone to the winery.'

'We did. I thought I should speak to Rafe about the harvest.'

'That must have been awkward for you,' said Phillipa, sitting down.

'Mmm. It was a bit.' Charlotte cast her mind back to Sally's appearance. 'But, it had to be done. And besides, I wanted to get all the papers concerning Five Oaks, just in case I decide to sell.' Charlotte folded the newspaper.

'But I thought you weren't interested in selling the winery.'

'I wasn't, but now...'

Phillipa eyed Charlotte. 'Don't tell me your change of mind is because of Rafe Simms. You ended that relationship almost two years ago, Charlotte. It shouldn't be a problem.' Charlotte did not reply. 'So, what else did you and Esme get up to while you were there?' continued Phillipa.

'Actually, we found something rather disturbing. In an old bureau that once belonged to Esme's fiancé, Thomas. Esme said that while Thomas was in Korea, she'd kept his letters there, in a small drawer. When she opened that drawer there were still letters inside, but not from Thomas. These were letters addressed to my mother. Three of them, sent anonymously, each telling her that Richard was seeing someone else. And they weren't written or typed, but made up from newspaper and magazine print.' Charlotte sighed. 'Poor Mum. Just when she and Richard were getting their lives back together. I wish I'd known.'

'Did you say there were *three* letters?'

'Yes.' Charlotte caught Phillipa's surprised look. 'Did you know about them, Phil?'

'I knew your mother had received one because I was there when she opened it. I didn't know there'd been others.' The words cut through Charlotte. 'Your mother made me promise not to say anything to anyone. And after her death... well, it had been so traumatic for everyone concerned that I didn't want to bring the matter up. I'm sorry, Charlotte. I should have said something, but the time never seemed right.' Phillipa paused. 'Where are the letters now?'

'They're at Esme's. I'm staying with her at the moment. I didn't like the thought of her being alone in the house after that break-in. I was going to tear the letters up, but Esme said we should give them to the police. Especially since Michael had said he was looking for letters when he went to Esme's that night.'

'I think Esme's right. The police need to be told, Charlotte, because they are asking questions about your mother. I know because they came to see me the other day.'

'Really? Well, I suppose that's because Michael told Esme he wanted to look through Mum's study.' Charlotte took a sip of her coffee not wanting to revisit thoughts of her mother's death. But perhaps now, with these letters surfacing, and Michael's death, she would have no choice.

'I take it they haven't spoken to you about her yet.' Charlotte shook her head. 'Well, they probably will.' Phillipa looked at her watch. 'Look, I have a meeting to attend so I'm going to have to go, but why don't we meet later for lunch.'

'I'd love to Phil, but I can't,' replied Charlotte. 'There's something I have to do. It's about that sketch I lent to Michael.'

'The Brandt sketch?'

'Yes. Apparently, Mum had been looking into its provenance before she died.'

'Well, that does surprise me because I believe she bought it from my boss, Aiden Maxwell, and he's nothing but reputable.'

'I don't know why she was doing it, but as I plan to sell the sketch I thought I'd follow it up.'

'Do you know how long and arduous a task that could be, Charlotte?'

'I can only imagine, but Mum did leave quite detailed notes about what she planned to do. I'll follow them as best I can.'

Phillipa smiled. 'Well, in my experience, enthusiasm is the first thing that goes so when it does, let me know and I'll give you a hand. And I won't tell Aiden. He'd be mortified if he knew your mother doubted him.'

Later that day, Charlotte made her way to Balgowlah and the home of Douglas Porteous in an effort to further her mother's research into the provenance of the Brandt sketch. She pulled over to the curb in front of a red brick Federation style semi, but hesitated before climbing out of the car. Unlike Claudia, Charlotte had little knowledge of the art world, and being unaware of what had transpired between her mother and Douglas Porteous when they met in 2010, she wanted to decide how to approach him. The house was situated on the low side of the street and on opening the front gate, she descended six steps into an immaculate front garden, its walk way bordered by white standard roses. Their scent filled the air around her as she made her way to the porch where she tentatively knocked on the front door. When it opened, she was greeted by a plump woman wearing a yellow floral dress, her curly grey hair framing a round smiling face. 'Can I help you?' she asked.

'My name's Charlotte Rossi. I'm looking for Douglas Porteous.' The woman's smile disappeared.'

'I'm Eunice Porteous. My husband died some time ago.'

'Oh. I'm sorry. I had no idea.'

'You weren't to know.' Eunice Porteous eyed Charlotte guardedly. 'What is it you wanted to see Douglas about? One of his orders that never got filled? If that's the case, then I'm very sorry. I probably didn't get in contact with all his customers at the time of his death.'

Charlotte shook her head. 'No, Mrs Porteous, it's nothing like that. It's about a piece of art work.'

'I beg your pardon?'

'A piece of art work. A sketch that my mother, Claudia Rossi, bought just before she died.'

Eunice Porteous folded her arms. 'Well, as I said, my husband is gone, and besides, he was a furniture maker. He wasn't an artist.'

'I'm not saying that he was, Mrs Porteous. According to this,' Charlotte held up the documentation her mother had left, 'your husband was the previous owner of a sketch. A Brandt sketch. And I understand that my mother came to see him about it in mid-June 2010.' Eunice Porteous tensed. 'She was making enquiries about its provenance, but unfortunately she died before she completed her task.'

'Well, as I said, you're mistaken. You have the wrong Porteous.'

I don't think so, thought Charlotte as she watched the door close in her face. Surprised as well as intrigued by Eunice Porteous's reaction at the mention of the Brandt sketch, Charlotte walked back through the garden to her car. Had her mother encountered a problem when she had approached Douglas Porteous? Is that why the report remained unfinished? Charlotte climbed into her car, opened the report and reread it. Aiden Maxwell's name caught her eye. She knew her mother had worked closely with Aiden on a number of projects. Surely she would have spoken to him about her concerns for the sketch's provenance. Charlotte started the car and as she did so, the sheer curtain on the main front window of Eunice Porteous's house moved. She's obviously frightened, but what of thought Charlotte?

Charlotte recognized Aiden Maxwell as soon as she walked into the Paddington gallery later that afternoon. 'Mr Maxwell,' she said as he glided across the room toward her. 'I'm Charlotte Rossi, Claudia Rossi's daughter.'

'Yes, of course. I remember you well, my dear,' he answered, a wide smile on his face. 'We met at a number of your mother's soirees.' Maxwell took Charlotte's hand and kissed it before adjusting his brilliant blue bow tie. 'How can I help? Are you interested in a particular piece?' he asked, looking round the room with his arm flung out.

'Not at the moment. Actually, Aiden, I've come to see you about a sketch that my mother purchased here. It's by an artist called Brandt.'

'And a very good choice it was too. I told her so at the time.'

'And I know she loved it. However, it's come to my attention that my mother wasn't satisfied with its provenance.'

Aiden Maxwell's smile left his face. 'Its provenance? But why?' Charlotte could feel Maxwell's growing agitation.

'That I don't know. I thought she might have spoken to you about it.'

'I wish she had.' Maxwell shook his head. 'This is most distressing. I don't know what to say, Charlotte, other than you let me look into the matter. You can appreciate, I'm sure, that my reputation is at stake here.'

'I'm sorry,' replied Charlotte. 'It wasn't my intention to create a problem. And I didn't expect you to have to look into the provenance yourself.'

'I'm more than happy to do so. After all, the gallery sold the painting to your mother. The least we can do is to put your mind at ease as to its authenticity.'

'Well in that case, I have a report here that mum was working on. It might help you get started.' Charlotte handed the report to

Aiden Maxwell. 'This afternoon, I spoke to Douglas Porteous's widow. Mr Porteous is mentioned in the report as a previous owner of the sketch. But Mrs Porteous denies her husband ever owned it.'

'I see. Well, I'll keep that in mind when I speak to her.'

❧CHAPTER 16❧

Fitzjohn and Betts stood at the whiteboard discussing their investigation when the Incident Room door opened and the Duty Sergeant appeared.

'There's someone here to see you, Chief Inspector,' he said. 'Marion Davies from the New South Wales Art Gallery. She says you're expecting her.'

'I am, Sergeant. Ask her to come in, will you?' As the Duty Sergeant left, Fitzjohn nodded to Betts who returned to his desk. Fitzjohn took his suit coat from the back of his chair and slipped it on before straightening his tie. As he did so, a plainly dressed woman, wearing dark rimmed glasses, came through the door. Her blue eyes darted between the two men before settling on Fitzjohn.

'I'm Detective Chief Inspector Fitzjohn, Ms Davies,' said Fitzjohn. 'And this is Detective Sergeant Betts.' Marian nodded at Betts as she sat down on the chair in front of Fitzjohn's desk. 'We appreciate your taking the time to come in to see us.'

'I was told at the gallery that you want to speak to me about Michael Rossi,' she said, putting her handbag on the floor next to her flat black shoes. 'I couldn't believe it when I heard about his death,' she continued. 'I'd been speaking to him only the day before.'

'So we understand,' said Fitzjohn. 'What time was that, exactly?'

'It was late in the afternoon. After four. Just before I left for the day.'

'And, can I ask what Michael Rossi wanted to see you about, Ms Davies?'

'Yes. He wanted to ask me about his sister, Claudia. He knew we'd worked together at the gallery, you see.'

'And how long had you and Claudia worked together?'

'We started at about the same time, so it was June 2003.'

'And you became friends?'

Marian Davies thought for a minute. 'I wouldn't say we were friends,' she said, pushing her glasses back up over the bridge of her nose. 'That is, Claudia never confided in me as friends might have occasion to do. No. I'd say we were colleagues.'

Fitzjohn sensed a level of indignation in Marian Davies voice. 'So you didn't meet socially.'

'No, Chief Inspector. The only social contact we ever had was at a dinner party Claudia held. At the time, I suspected I was invited to make up numbers.' Marian smoothed down her grey skirt. 'In fact, that dinner party was what Michael Rossi wanted to talk to me about last Friday afternoon.'

'Oh?'

'Yes. You see, at the time, Claudia had asked me what I thought of a sketch she'd recently purchased. It was by Brandt. You may have heard of Brandt, but if not he was one of the 20th century's leading figures in art. You only have to observe his creativity that is manifested in the variety of mediums that he used. That's why, after close examination... Well, it was rather embarrassing, really, because I knew Claudia had spent a lot of money purchasing the sketch, but for that very reason I felt it necessary to tell her that it was a fake.'

'And did you tell Mr Rossi this when he came to see you last Friday afternoon?'

'I did, but he said he'd already been told of that fact that very afternoon. What he wanted from me was the name of the art dealer who'd sold the sketch to Claudia.'

'And were you able to tell him who it was?'

'Oh, yes. Claudia mentioned the dealer's name when I told her the sketch was a fake. And, of course, being in the art business, I know of him. His name's Aiden Maxwell.' Fitzjohn sat forward in his chair. 'He has a gallery in Paddington. Claudia used to do restoration work for him from time to time.'

Marian Davies face gaped. 'You don't think Michael's death… I'll never forgive myself if my telling him the dealer's name has led to his death.'

'Tell me, Ms Davies, in your opinion, were the irregularities in the sketch easy to detect?'

'In this case not necessarily, Chief Inspector. I just happen to be an expert on Brandt's work, and it was only the finest discrepancies I noticed.'

'I see.' Fitzjohn paused. 'When was this dinner party, Ms Davies?'

'Sometime in June 2010, as I remember. Not long before Claudia died, as a matter of fact.'

'And do you know whether she contacted Aiden Maxwell about the possibility that the sketch was a fake?'

'I have no idea, Chief Inspector. Claudia never said.'

'Did Michael Rossi ask you anything else?'

'No. But he did tell me something. Something unsettling.' Marian Davies took a breath. 'He told me Claudia had been murdered because of the Brandt sketch.'

<hr />

After Marian Davies departure, Fitzjohn glanced over at Betts, who still sat writing in his notebook. 'Well, Betts, Ms Davies has managed to turn our investigation on its head.'

'She has, sir,' said Betts, closing his notebook. 'The very fact Michael Rossi believed his sister was murdered, fits in with what we've got so far. We know he received a telephone call from Robert Nesbit on Friday afternoon telling him of Richard Edwards failing health, and that Mr Edwards wanted to talk to Rossi about Claudia. This caused the victim to leave the winery earlier than expected. We also know the approximate time that the victim visited Richard Edwards in St Vincent's Hospital. Around 3:30pm that same afternoon where, we presume, he was told not only that the sketch was a fake, but that Claudia's death had not been accidental, but murder.' Betts tapped his pen on his notebook. 'Maybe that's why he wanted to speak to his solicitor, David Spencer, about Claudia's life insurance policy. After all, it'd been paid out, and if she had been murdered...'

'Mmm. Sounds feasible,' replied Fitzjohn. 'We'll work on that premise and also that Claudia Rossi's death was suspicious, unless we find out otherwise.' Fitzjohn put his glasses on, smoothed down his wispy hair, and rose from his chair. 'I want to have another word with Aiden Maxwell.' Fitzjohn slipped his suit coat on. 'But before we do, let's talk to Charlotte Rossi again. You never know, she might be able to add something to all this.'

———

Fitzjohn and Betts stepped into Charlotte Rossi's Double Bay bookshop later that same day. Housed in a Federation style building, its atmosphere of old-world charm and clutter, blended with the smell of paper, leather and dust, lent a comfortable air.

'Hello, Chief Inspector,' came a voice from the back of the shop. Fitzjohn looked between the shelves to see Esme Timmons sitting at a desk in front of a computer screen, an enquiring look on her face. 'I expect you're looking for Charlotte.'

'We are, Miss Timmons,' answered Fitzjohn, making his way between the shelving to where Esme sat.

'Well, you'll be disappointed because she's out, and I'm not sure when she'll be back. I'm spending the day here, assisting Irene with some cataloging. It keeps "the grey matter" alive. I don't suppose you have news about my perfume bottle.'

'Not yet, Miss Timmons.'

'Oh, well, I'm glad you've dropped by anyway because there's something I think you should see. It concerns Claudia... and perhaps Michael.' Esme opened her handbag and brought out the three letters that she and Charlotte had found in the bureau at the winery. She handed them to Fitzjohn. 'As you can see, they're letters all addressed to Claudia.' Esme recounted the finding of the letters. 'They're content is disturbing to say the least, Chief Inspector. I think you'd describe them as poison pen letters. I wondered if they might be what Michael was looking for when he came to see me on Friday evening, but I suppose we'll never know for sure.'

Fitzjohn removed one of the letters from its envelope and ran his eyes over the text, each individual letter cut from what looked like magazine print. 'You're right, Miss Timmons, they are disturbing.' While he studied the letter, Esme disclosed details of Claudia's life that might prompt such prose. At the same time, Phillipa Braithwaite's words about Claudia's, seemingly tumultuous relationship with Richard Edwards, came into Fitzjohn's thoughts. 'So, Claudia's relationship with her partner, Richard Edwards, was strained at one point, Miss Timmons,' Fitzjohn said at last.

'Very much so, Chief Inspector. Richard had a fancy woman during the time they were together. I don't know who she was. Nobody did. It caused him and Claudia to separate for a time, but then they patched things up. Or so I thought until these letters turned up.' Esme sighed. 'Poor Claudia. I only wish she'd told me. What sort of a mind, do you suppose stoops so low as to concoct such rubbish.'

'A disturbed one, Miss Timmons.' Fitzjohn put the letter back into its envelope before looking at each of the three envelopes. 'Not handwritten, but, it would seem, hand delivered. There aren't any post marks. I'll take these with me if you don't mind, Miss Timmons. They may help us with our investigation.'

'I hope they do,' said Esme.

'Talking about Claudia, Miss Timmons, can you tell me anything about a sketch that she owned?'

'The only sketch I know of is one by Arthur Brandt. It was left to Charlotte in her mother's will. Charlotte plans to sell it.' Esme paused. 'Why do you ask?'

'Because it's come to our attention that there's a problem with it, Miss Timmons.'

'I know. When Charlotte and I were tidying up after the break-in, we found a report that Claudia had written concerning its provenance. I don't pretend to know anything about such matters, Chief Inspector, but I do know that it's important, if one plans to sell a piece of art, that the provenance is intact, or there's a legitimate reason why it isn't. And according to Claudia's report, it's obvious she had her doubts.' Esme paused. 'I suppose even an expert can be fooled. I wouldn't be surprised if it does turn out to be a fake. I mean, why else would Claudia be looking into its provenance?'

'You're very perceptive, Miss Timmons, because we've reason to believe that that's the case. Do you know where the sketch is now?'

'It's at my house in Waverton. Charlotte brought it with her when she came to stay. It had been at Michael's before that. She'd lent it to him because she didn't care for it. Too modern for her taste, I suspect. I told her she could leave it in her mother's study while she arranges for its sale. Can I ask your particular interest in the sketch, Chief Inspector? Is it because it's a fake or does it have some connection to Michael's death?'

Unaccustomed to discussing his investigations openly with anyone other than his team of investigators, Fitzjohn, nevertheless, felt drawn to answering Esme Timmons's question. Why was that? Her enquiring mind and pragmatism? Yes, but there was something else, he thought as he looked into those bright blue eyes. It was Esme's unmistakable zest for life. Even when she had just suffered the loss of yet another member of her family. One more blow in her long life. 'We're led to believe that your nephew went to see someone at the New South Wales Art Gallery last Friday afternoon, Miss Timmons, to ask about the sketch,' he answered at last.

'Oh, I see. So, it's quite possible Michael was looking for Claudia's report as well as letters when he came to see me last Friday evening. Mmm.'

'Where's the report now, Miss Timmons?' asked Fitzjohn.

'Charlotte has it. As I mentioned before, she plans to speak to the previous owner of the sketch.' Esme frowned. 'But that might not be a good idea if it's a fake as you say. Oh dear.'

<hr />

Fitzjohn eased himself into the passenger seat of the car and watched Betts climb in beside him, his arms loaded with books. 'It looks like you made use of your time in there, Betts.'

'Used bookshops, sir. I love them.' Betts placed the books on the back seat of the car. At the same time, Fitzjohn's mobile phone rang.

'Fitzjohn here. *I beg your pardon?*' Fitzjohn stared out over the hood of the car as Betts pulled away from the curb.

'Is it bad news about the tree, sir?' he asked, maneuvering his way into the traffic.

'I wish it was. That was the Duty Officer at Day Street Police Station. Sophie's in the *nick*.'

'She's *what?*' said Betts, grinding into third gear.

'Just what I said.' Fitzjohn looked across at Betts. 'She was arrested this morning at the university sit in.' Fitzjohn's eyes narrowed. 'Do I denote amusement in your face, Betts?'

'Not in the least, sir. Sophie must be very upset.'

'To hell with Sophie,' barked Fitzjohn. 'I'm upset. Can you imagine what my life will be like if her mother finds out?' Fitzjohn sighed. 'There's nothing for it. I'll have to bail Sophie out.'

{CHAPTER 17}

Fitzjohn arrived at Kings Cross Police Station later that afternoon in an uncharacteristically tense mood. He found Betts and Reynolds in the Incident Room standing at the whiteboard, discussing the case.

'Is Sophie all right?' asked Betts as Fitzjohn sat down in his chair.

'I daresay her pride is hurt, but otherwise, I believe, she's faring better than me right now, Betts. I've left her to watch the tree branch that's now scraping the top of my greenhouse.' Fitzjohn opened his briefcase and took his papers out. 'She has strict instructions to call me if it snaps.' Fitzjohn sighed. 'It's distressing bailing one's niece out of gaol.'

Reynolds, sensing Fitzjohn chagrin, glanced at Betts before he said, 'I was just about to get a cup of coffee, sir, would you like one?'

'I don't know about coffee. I think I need a stiff drink,' replied Fitzjohn, 'but coffee will be fine. Thanks, Reynolds.'

'Perhaps it's just as well Edith and I weren't blessed with children,' said Fitzjohn as Reynolds left the room. 'I doubt I'd have coped.' He removed his pen from his breast pocket and tossed it on to his desk. 'How are things here, anyway? Have you been able to contact Charlotte Rossi about that sketch?'

'I tried, sir, but she still hasn't returned to the bookshop. I'll try again later.'

'Do that, because I have a feeling that sketch is about to become central to our investigation. Not only because of Michael Rossi's death, but the death of his sister as well. Anything more on those death cap mushrooms?'

'Yes, sir. The New South Wales Art Gallery has confirmed that Claudia Rossi was in Canberra in July, 2010. She went there to do some work at The National Art Gallery. I'm just waiting for the exact dates she was there.'

'Ah. So, if it's found that Claudia was in Canberra just prior to when she fell ill, there's every possibility she came by the mushroom herself. Perhaps brought them home with her for dinner.' Fitzjohn paused. 'It's a chilling thought.'

'But it doesn't fit with what Michael Rossi told Ms Davies, sir. That his sister had been murdered because of the Brandt sketch.'

'That's true. Which is why we have to look for other ways she could have come by them. We'll start with Aiden Maxwell. Have him brought in for questioning, Betts.' As Fitzjohn spoke, Williams put his head around the Incident Room door.

'Ah, Williams, come in,' said Fitzjohn sitting forward expectantly. 'News on Douglas Porteous, I hope.'

'Yes, sir. Apparently, Mr Porteous died in July, 2010. At around about the same time as Claudia Rossi, but from natural causes. A massive stroke, apparently.'

'Thank goodness for that,' said Fitzjohn, slumping back in his chair.

'He's survived by his wife, Eunice Porteous, who still lives in the family home in North Balgowlah.'

'Right, well, it's not ideal but we'll speak to Mrs Porteous.'

Fitzjohn and Williams made their way to North Balgowlah a short time later, pulling up in front of a neat, red brick semi-detached house where a middle-aged woman stood pruning white standard roses that bordered the garden path. She stopped when Fitzjohn and Williams approached, her gloved hands falling to her sides, her expression wary.

'Can I help you?'

'Mrs Porteous?' asked Fitzjohn, sensing the woman's nervous disposition.

'Yes.'

Fitzjohn held up his warrant card. 'I'm Detective Chief Inspector Fitzjohn. This is Detective Senior Sergeant Williams. We're from the New South Wales Police. We'd like to ask you a few questions, if we may, about your late husband, Douglas Porteous.'

'Douglas?' Eunice Porteous looked around furtively displaying her nervousness. 'We'd better speak inside then.' Removing her gardening gloves and placing them, along with her secateurs, on the lower step of the front porch, she led the way into the house. 'We can sit in here,' she said ushering Fitzjohn and Williams into a small living room overlooking the front garden. 'I take it that young woman, Charlotte Rossi, reported me to the police,' she said as they sat down.

Fitzjohn gave Eunice Porteous a quizzical look. 'No. We haven't heard from Ms Rossi. But I daresay we're here about the same matter. A sketch that we understand your late husband once owned?' Eunice Porteous shifted in her chair. 'Is that the case, Mrs Porteous?'

'No, it isn't, Chief Inspector.'

'I see. Then can you tell us your husband's connection to the sketch? I take it there is one.'

'There is, but it's a long and complicated story,' replied Eunice Porteous.

'We have the time to listen, Mrs Porteous.' Fitzjohn sat back on the sofa. 'Perhaps you can start by telling us what happened when Charlotte Rossi came to see you.'

'Well, like you, she was under the impression that Douglas was the previous owner. I told her I didn't know what she was talking about. I've since had second thoughts. It's been bothering me all day.'

'Why is that, Mrs Porteous?'

'Because I wished I'd told her not to pursue the matter, Chief Inspector. The reason being that I think it's one of the reasons my husband is dead.'

'But we've been led to believe your husband died of a stroke.'

'He did, but there's no doubt in my mind it was brought on by what happened in the week prior to his death, and culminated the night his workshop burned to the ground. I think that was the end for him. Everything Doug had worked for all his life, gone. The fire was found to be caused by an electrical fault, but at the time, as far as the insurance company was concerned, there was every possibility my husband had started the fire. And that meant a long and protracted investigation.'

'But I'm getting ahead of myself. I should digress to what happened before the fire.' Eunice Porteous pressed her lips together before she continued. 'I told Ms Rossi that she had the wrong Porteous. That my husband was a furniture maker, not an artist. That wasn't true, of course. He was an artist who, unwittingly, became involved with an unscrupulous art dealer who offered to market and sell his work. Initially, Doug was pleased. How could he not be? To have someone in the art world the slightest bit interested in his work pleased him no end. But all too soon that pleasure came to an end.'

'Why? What happened?' asked Fitzjohn.

'Well, you see, Chief Inspector. Much of Doug's work was copying old masters as well as other well known artists. He didn't realise anything was wrong until the day Claudia Rossi came to see him. She also believed he was the previous owner of a Brandt sketch she had recently purchased. She didn't know that it was one of Doug's reproductions. Brandt's name had been surreptitiously added to the work and Doug's name included in a long provenance. Mrs Rossi said she was looking into the sketch's provenance because she'd been told by an expert that it was a fake. She asked my husband if he'd be prepared to support her if this turned out to be true. I'll never forget Doug's face. He was mortified. The thought he was involved in art fraud, albeit, without his knowledge, was more than he could bear. Not to mention his embarrassment at having to tell this woman that she was right. It was a copy, and he was the artist. It all but destroyed him, Chief Inspector.' Eunice Porteous blinked back her tears. 'His reputation, as far as he was concerned, was sullied, and that afternoon he went to see the art dealer who'd sold the sketch to Claudia Rossi.'

'What was this art dealer's name?' asked Fitzjohn.

'Aiden Maxwell,' said Eunice slowly. Williams looked up from his notebook and caught Fitzjohn's eye. 'He has a gallery in Paddington.'

'And was he the dealer who had approached your husband earlier?'

'No. That man's name was Bernard Wilson. I still have the card he left, but it won't be much good to you. The contact details are false.'

'What was Aiden Maxwell's reaction when your husband confronted him?' asked Fitzjohn.

'Doug said he appeared in utter shock, but then he would be, wouldn't he? Whether he'd sold that copy as authentic or not.' Eunice paused. 'He told Doug he'd acquired the sketch from another dealer, and would look into the matter immediately. Of course, there was no way of knowing whether he was telling the truth so my husband suggested they report the matter to the police.'

'And what was Aiden Maxwell's response to that?'

'Maxwell agreed, and they made arrangements to meet the next day, but that night Doug's studio burnt to the ground and events took over. A few days later, Doug had a stroke and died.'

'Did you hear from Aiden Maxwell again?'

'No. Not a word. And I wasn't surprised. After all, if Aiden Maxwell was mixed up in the fraud, he would have been counting his blessings when Doug didn't contact him again. And even if he wasn't involved, I imagine he'd welcome the opportunity to sweep the whole affair under the rug. Let's face it, Chief Inspector, that sort of publicity wouldn't do his business any good.' Eunice Porteous sighed. 'Needless to say, when Charlotte Rossi turned up here this morning and told me who she was, and that her mother had also died in 2010... well, quite frankly, I panicked.'

'I can appreciate that, Mrs Porteous, but how do you feel now? Would you be willing to give us a description of the man who approached your husband initially?'

'I'm certainly willing, Chief Inspector, but I don't know how helpful my description will be. It was quite a while ago but I do remember that he had one of those charismatic personalities that draws you in, so to speak. No wonder Doug was fooled by his performance.'

'And his physical description. Can you tell us what he looked like?' asked Fitzjohn.

'Well, he looked to be in his forties. Of average height. Quite a good-looking man as I remember. And I might be mistaken, but I think he had blue eyes.'

———

Fitzjohn and Williams left Eunice Porteous to continue her pruning in the early evening light. 'Seems there's no real closure to this for Eunice Porteous, sir,' said Williams, getting into the car. 'She's a nervous wreck.'

'Well, let's hope we can help to change that for her, Williams, although I don't think it's going to be easy. It seems to me that Aiden Maxwell could be unaware that the Brandt sketch is a copy. On the other hand, if he was mixed up in that art fraud, he's the person who'll be able to tell us who approached Douglas Porteous.'

———

With the last vestiges of light disappearing below the horizon of city buildings, Fitzjohn and Williams entered Kings Cross

Police Station and made their way to the Incident Room where they found Betts writing feverishly in his notebook.

'Were you able to catch up with Charlotte Rossi, Betts?' asked Fitzjohn.

'I wanted to wait until I spoke to you first, sir, because I've come across something concerning Ms Rossi.'

'Oh, what's that?' Fitzjohn sat down at his desk.

'Well, I've been checking out everyone who was close to Claudia Rossi. Her partner Richard Edwards, her best friend Phillipa Braithwaite, and her daughter, Charlotte. In doing so, I've found that in 2010, the year Claudia died, Charlotte Rossi lived in Adelaide. At the time, she was studying for a Bachelor of Viticulture and Oenology at the University of Adelaide. Viticulture being the study of grapes and oenology being the study of all aspect of wine and winemaking.'

'I know what viticulture and oenology are, Betts. Wouldn't someone taking on such a degree have an interest in becoming a winemaker?'

'It's a four-year course, so I think you'd have to be fairly committed, sir. Charlotte Rossi was in her last year at the time of her mother's death.'

'And did she complete her degree?'

'Yes. At the end of 2010.'

'And here we are in 2012 and she's running a bookshop. I wonder what happened to her aspirations to work in the wine industry. Especially since, at the time, she owned half a winery.'

'And now with her uncle's death she'll own the winery outright,' added Betts.

'Isn't Adelaide another one of the few places in Australia where death cap mushrooms are found?'

'Yes sir.'

Fitzjohn sat tapping his pen on his desk. 'Anything else?'

'There's also Phillipa Braithwaite. We already know she manages Aiden Maxwell's gallery in Carlton, Melbourne, so presumably she must journey there fairly regularly to carry out her duties.'

'And Melbourne and its suburbs are also a source for death cap mushrooms,' added Fitzjohn. 'I can see where this is leading, Betts. If it turns out that Claudia Rossi didn't bring those mushrooms back to Sydney herself, there are others who could have.'

'With the possible intent to kill Claudia Rossi,' added Betts.

'It's a chilling thought, and one I'd like to lay to rest,' said Fitzjohn. 'We'll start by speaking to Charlotte Rossi, but we'll do it first thing in the morning. It's late and I want to get home. Apparently, Sophie phoned the station while I was out. I want to see if I still have a greenhouse.'

❧CHAPTER 18❧

Fitzjohn and Betts arrived at the bookshop early the following morning to find Charlotte Rossi wrestling with the lock on the front door. 'Good morning, Ms Rossi,' said Fitzjohn.

Charlotte looked over her shoulder. 'Morning, Chief Inspector. I shan't be long,' she said wincing. 'This lock is so old it tends to stick first thing in the morning.'

'Here, let me try, Ms Rossi,' offered Betts, smiling. Betts's efforts saw the door fly open.

'Thank you, Sergeant.' Charlotte, with a polite smile, made her way into the bookshop's quiet atmosphere and placed a large canvas bag on her desk.

'I trust Miss Timmons told you we spoke to her yesterday,' said Fitzjohn, making his way between the shelves.

'Yes, she did. She said you were asking after the Brandt sketch so I brought it in with me. I had planned to drop it off at the police station later today.' Charlotte Rossi gestured to the canvas bag.

'I also have the report you asked about. The one my mother was compiling into its provenance.' Charlotte rummaged in her handbag and handed the report to Fitzjohn. 'Perhaps I should mention that I gave a copy of that to the art dealer who sold my mother the sketch. He said he'd look into the provenance for me.'

'Aiden Maxwell?' asked Fitzjohn.

'Yes. Do you know of him?'

'His name's been raised in the course of our enquiries, Ms Rossi. Would you say that Mr Maxwell was well acquainted with your mother?'

'Yes. Other than doing quite a bit of work for him, she and Mr Maxwell met socially.' Charlotte paused. 'I'm sure he wouldn't have knowingly sold a fake piece of art work to Mum.' Charlotte looked at the canvas bag containing the sketch. 'Do you think Michael's death had something to do with this sketch, Chief Inspector?' She caught Fitzjohn's eye. 'Silly question. Of course, you must. Why else would you be interested in it.'

'I'm afraid I'm not at liberty to go into it at this time, Ms Rossi, but what I can say is, we are also looking into your mother's activities just prior to her becoming ill. And, in so doing, it would help us greatly if you could tell us who she would have come into contact with around that time.'

'That's difficult because I spent much of my time in Adelaide in 2010. I was studying there.'

'Well, perhaps you can start by telling us where you were when your mother became ill.'

'As a matter of fact, I was here in New South Wales then on a semester break. Staying with a friend in the Hunter Valley.'

'And how long had you been there?'

'Actually, I'd only just arrived. Prior to that I'd been at Mum's.'

'And how long were you at your mother's?'

'I only spent one night. It was a Friday. I left the following morning. I think around seven-thirty.' Charlotte fidgeted with her bracelet. 'Mum and I had words, Chief Inspector.'

'Ah. I see. Can I ask the name of the friend you stayed with, in the Hunter Valley?'

Charlotte tucked her fair hair behind her ears. 'It was someone I was engaged to at the time. Rafe Simms.'

A hint of surprise came to Fitzjohn's face. 'The winemaker who recently took over the harvest at Five Oaks Winery?' Betts looked up from his notebook.

'Yes. That's right.'

'I see. Do you know if your mother planned to see anyone after you left for the winery?'

'She did say that her partner, Richard, was due back from Singapore that Saturday morning. But that's the only thing I can remember her mentioning. Except for Phillipa, of course.'

'Phillipa Braithwaite,' asked Fitzjohn.

'Yes.'

'Do you know if your mother had seen Phillipa Braithwaite during that week?'

'No, I don't. I just remember Mum mentioning a conversation they'd had the day before I arrived. I'm afraid that's all I know. With being away in Adelaide most of the year, I never kept up with Mum's comings and goings.'

'That's okay, Ms Rossi. There's just one other matter you might be able to assist us with. We understand your mother became ill after ingesting death cap mushrooms. Was it her practice, given the opportunity, to pick wild mushrooms?'

Charlotte hesitated and fidgeted with the ring on her right hand. 'I hate talking about this,' she said at last, 'but yes. It was something she'd always done as far back as I can remember. Mum walked early each morning whether she was at home in Sydney or at the winery, and I know she'd pick mushrooms if she came across them.'

'Do you think she would have done so when she was away on business? Say in Canberra.'

'Oh. This question came up at the Coroner's inquest,' replied Charlotte. 'And, although it couldn't be proved, it was decided that because Mum was in the habit of picking wild mushrooms, she could have gathered them in the morning before she left Canberra.' Charlotte paused. 'It was also thought that as death cap mushrooms aren't found in New South Wales, she might not have been aware that they were poisonous. Of course, Michael was irate at that assumption.'

'Why?'

'He argued that there was no way that Mum would have misjudged mushrooms that she picked. He maintained she'd been murdered.'

'And what do you think, Ms Rossi? About the mushrooms, that is?'

'I think my mother made a mistake that morning, Chief Inspector.'

Fitzjohn and Betts left Charlotte and made their way back to their car. 'I can't see Charlotte Rossi as a suspect, sir.'

'Why, Betts? Because she's too attractive. Don't let that fact cloud your judgment.' Betts put the sketch on to the back seat and closed the door. 'I know it's unpleasant,' said Fitzjohn, 'but Charlotte Rossi has to remain a person of interest in our investigation until we find out how Claudia Rossi came by those mushrooms. How many hours did you say it is before death cap mushrooms take effect on the human body?'

'Approximately sixteen hours before the first bout of sickness, sir.'

'Mmm. So, if Claudia was admitted to hospital early on Saturday morning, one would assume she'd eaten the mushrooms during the day on Friday,' said Fitzjohn as he settled himself into the passenger seat of the car.

'Or possibly late on Thursday evening, sir, after she arrived back from Canberra. After all, if she'd gone to the trouble to pick the mushrooms, you'd think she'd have thought the fresher the better. However, if that was the case, I think she would have been feeling ill on the Friday evening.'

'What time did Charlotte Rossi say she arrived at her mother's place?'

'Around noon on Friday, sir. She left around seven-thirty on Saturday morning. So her mother was very likely feeling ill and either never mentioned it or...'

'Or Charlotte Rossi knew very well what was troubling her mother and wanted to leave before things got worse,' said Fitzjohn.

'Where to now, sir?'

'The Hunter Valley, Betts. I think it's time we made Rafe Simms's acquaintance.'

{CHAPTER 19}

A little after two o'clock that same day, Fitzjohn and Betts arrived in the Hunter Valley and after passing through the town of Cessnock, continued on into the rolling countryside. Fitzjohn sat quietly, immersed in his thoughts. Not of the investigation, but of the few precious days he and Edith had spent in the Hunter Valley to celebrate her winning Grand Champion at the North Shore Orchid Society Spring Show. Little interested in orchids at the time, Fitzjohn now wished he had appreciated what this award had meant to Edith.

'This is it, sir,' said Betts, slowing the car. 'Peppertree Grove Wines.' Brought back from his thoughts, Fitzjohn peered out of the passenger car window as they drove beneath the wrought iron archway and followed the road that led to a nestle of buildings. '*Taste our wines in the Cellar Door and Restaurant. Enjoy wine tasting, cheeses and other gourmet products,*' said Betts, reading the sign. 'Too bad we can't partake.' Leaving their car, they made their way beneath the wisteria covered courtyard, its fragrance following them into the crowded Cellar Door.

'Can I guide you through our range of wines, sir?' said a young woman who stood behind the counter, her bright smile adding to the convivial atmosphere. 'Unless, of course, you have something specific you'd like to taste.'

'Actually, we're here to see Mr Simms,' said Fitzjohn.

'Oh, I'm sorry. You must be Mr Roland from the Wine Grapes Marketing Board. Rafe's expecting you.' Before Fitzjohn could reply, the young woman looked further along the counter to a tall man pouring wine for a group of tourists. 'Rafe, darling, your visitors are here.' Rafe Simms approached offering his hand. 'Mr Roland.'

'I'm afraid there's been a bit of confusion, Mr Simms,' said Fitzjohn. 'I'm Detective Chief Inspector Fitzjohn and this is Detective Sergeant Betts. We're from the New South Wales Police.' Fitzjohn looked around the room. 'I realise you're busy, but it is necessary that we speak to you.'

'About Michael Rossi, is it?' asked Rafe Simms.

'Yes.'

'Then I think we might walk over to the house, Chief Inspector. It'll be quieter there.'

Once outside, Fitzjohn and Betts followed Rafe Simms along a gravel path that led through a copse of peppercorn trees to a sandstone bungalow, its wide verandah providing a stunning vista across the valley, and the mountain range beyond. Rafe gestured to a group of wicker chairs. 'We can talk here, Chief Inspector.'

With the cooling effect of a soft breeze, Fitzjohn settled himself into one of the chairs. 'It's a beautiful spot, Mr Simms,' he said.

Rafe Simms smiled. 'It is, but I can't take any credit. Most of what you see was established by my grandfather more than 50

years ago, including many of our finest vines.' Rafe Simms sat
back in his chair stretching his long legs before him. 'Of course,
much has been added as we've acquired more land.'

'Is Five Oaks Winery such a big operation?' asked Fitzjohn.

'No. It's what we call a boutique winery, but it does produce
high quality wines. In fact, it's won some very prestigious awards
in the last few years.'

'Oh? Is that to the credit of Pierce Whitehead?'

'Yes. He's an excellent winemaker. That's why I thought it was
a shame that he and Michael didn't get on. And as far as Michael
is concerned, I don't know that I can add much to what I told the
police when they came to see me, Chief Inspector.'

'I realise that, Mr Simms. Actually, we're here to ask you about
Michael Rossi's sister, Claudia.' Rafe Simms gave Fitzjohn a questioning look. 'We're trying to piece together who she came into
contact with in the days leading up to her admittance to hospital.'

'Why? Do you think her death had something to do with
Michael's?'

'That's what we're trying to find out.'

'Well, I don't know how much help I can be. Claudia wasn't a
person I came into contact with much.' Rafe hesitated. 'In fact, if
the truth be known, she wanted as little to do with me as possible.
Especially after Charlotte and I became engaged.'

'Can I ask why?'

'It was because of a particularly nasty incident that happened
years ago involving my father.' Rafe caught Fitzjohn's expectant
look. 'He left Claudia at 'the altar. Literally.'

'They were to be married?'

'Yes. And if that wasn't enough, he married my mother the
following week. So, I could understand why Claudia didn't want

me marrying her daughter, but that doesn't mean to say it made it easy for Charlotte and me.'

'I shouldn't imagine it would,' said Fitzjohn. 'But Claudia got her wish in the end. You and Charlotte didn't marry.'

'No.' Rafe Simms paused. 'We tried not to let Claudia's opinion of me and my family affect our relationship, but inevitably it did. I think mainly because when Claudia died, Charlotte had to cope with not only her grief, but also guilt. She and Claudia had been close at one time. Our engagement created a rift between them that was never resolved. Of course, Michael's views on how Claudia died didn't help Charlotte either.'

'He didn't agree with the Coroner's finding?' asked Fitzjohn.

'Far from it. He made that clear on a number of occasions. Usually when we were sitting here tasting wines. And what he said was rather disturbing. You see, Michael was convinced Claudia had been deliberately poisoned.'

'Did he say why he felt so strongly about it?' asked Fitzjohn.

'It was something along the lines that Claudia would be alive today if she had attended the dinner party he'd invited her to that week.'

'Did he say when this dinner engagement was?'

'I seem to remember it was the night she got back from a business trip to Canberra. Just a couple of days before she died.' Betts glanced over at Fitzjohn.

'Did he say why Claudia declined his invitation?'

'No.' Rafe Simms paused. 'Anyway, after Claudia's death, Charlotte returned to Adelaide to complete her studies. We had planned to be married that following summer, but after she returned from Adelaide in November of that year, she did a complete turn-around. She bought the bookshop in Double Bay with money her mother left her. I travelled down to Sydney as often as I could, but eventually she told me she'd changed her mind. She no longer wished to get married.'

———⊷⊶———

'So, according to Rafe Simms,' said Fitzjohn as they drove back along the road leading from Peppertree Grove Wines, 'Claudia declined the victim's invitation to his dinner party on the day she returned from Canberra. The Thursday before she died.' Fitzjohn paused. 'I seem to remember Phillipa Braithwaite told us that Claudia had cancelled their dinner engagement on that same Thursday evening? In favour of what, I wonder?'

'Maybe she was tired after driving back from Canberra that day, sir. After all, it's over 300 kilometers.'

'Possibly. Or, if she had picked those mushrooms while she was there, she might have decided to stay at home and eat,' added Fitzjohn. Fitzjohn thought for a moment. 'Take me through, again, what you know about these death cap mushrooms, Betts. Didn't you say that they can take up to sixteen hours to take effect?'

'Yes, sir. And as Claudia Rossi was hospitalized early on the Saturday morning, there are two possibilities. Either she was poisoned on Thursday evening after returning from Canberra, or up to lunchtime on the Friday.'

———⊷⊶———

Lightning flashed in the night sky as Fitzjohn climbed out of the taxi and into the warm, humid atmosphere. Turning toward his cottage, he collected the mail from the letterbox beside the gate, and made his way along the path to the front door. Once inside, the aroma of food filled the air and he smiled to himself, remembering the almost forgotten warm feeling of coming home to someone. He found Sophie in the kitchen glued to the television.

'All's well with the tree branch, I take it,' he said, placing his briefcase on the kitchen table.

'It was the last time I looked, Uncle Alistair, but the weather bureau says we're going to get a storm tonight.'

'I know, and it looks like it's arrived.' Fitzjohn peered out of the rain splattered kitchen window. 'What smells so delicious?'

'It's my favourite dish,' said Sophie. 'Mainly because it's the only one I know how to cook with any kind of success. Chicken in Paprika with Lime.'

'Sounds complicated.' Fitzjohn removed his suit coat and rested it over the back of a kitchen chair. 'I want to talk to you about your arrest before we sit down to dinner, Sophie, and about your mother.'

Sophie scrambled to her feet. 'You're not going to tell Mum are you, Uncle Alistair? Please don't. My life won't be worth living if you do. You know what she's like. She'll make me transfer to Melbourne University and live at home. I'd wither and die. My youth sapped away.'

'No need to be melodramatic,' replied Fitzjohn. 'If you think about it, returning to Melbourne might be your best option. After all, being arrested doesn't seem to me to be a very good way of conducting your independent life. Does it?'

'No, it doesn't. It's been the worst day of my life, but I believe I have learnt from the whole horrible experience. Doesn't that count for anything?'

Fitzjohn looked at his only niece, and goddaughter, her large brown eyes imploring him into collusion against her mother. But could he blame her? After all, Meg's devotion to duty as both Sophie's mother and his sister was nothing short of stifling. 'I'll have to think about it,' he said.

'Oh, thank you,' Uncle Alistair. 'You're wonderful. Now, dinner won't be for about half an hour so I'll pour you a whisky, shall I?'

'You don't have to go overboard, Sophie. As I said, I have to think about it. But a shot of whisky wouldn't go astray.' Fitzjohn took his newspaper out of his briefcase and made his way into the conservatory where he settled himself into his leather chair.

'*Oh, no,*' screamed Sophie.

'What is it?' Fitzjohn jumped up from his chair and returned to the kitchen.

'*Look!* I'm on the ABC news. If mum sees this my life will be well and truly over.' Sophie slumped down on to a kitchen chair.

'As will mine,' said Fitzjohn as if to himself. 'And what's more, I've got a feeling that in a minute or two that phone's going to ring.' As Fitzjohn said the words, the wall phone rang.

'You'd better answer it, my girl,' he said, turning back toward the conservatory.

'Couldn't you, Uncle Alistair? You're so much better at dealing with mum than I am. And obviously, she wants to speak to you. After all, she wouldn't expect me to be here.'

'No. She thinks you're in gaol.' Fitzjohn groaned and picked up the receiver.

'Hello? Meg dear... Yes, she was... Meg, if you will just listen to me for a... No, Sophie isn't in gaol. I bailed her out this afternoon. She's just... Calm yourself down, Meg. Getting upset isn't going to change the fact that your daughter was arrested.

Yes, it is unfortunate, but it happened, so we just have to live with...' A creaking noise followed by a crash and breaking glass stopped Fitzjohn in mid-stream. With the phone still to his ear, he peered through the kitchen window. 'My god. The greenhouse. Here, speak to your mother,' he yelled, tossing the phone to Sophie before running from the room. Outside, buffeted by the howling wind as it whipped through what remained of the flowerbeds bordering the garden path, Fitzjohn lifted his gaze to the jagged, grotesque remains of the greenhouse, the tree branch now resting inside. Transfixed, as the rain dripped from his chin, Fitzjohn's shoulders slumped inside his sodden suit, 'I'm sorry, Edith,' he said.

❊CHAPTER 20❊

A sense of urgency filled Fitzjohn as he walked into the Incident Room the following morning where members of his investigative team anticipated the start of the case management meeting. Amid the din, he made his way to his desk and sat down before catching Betts's eye. 'Sorry I'm late,' he said, methodically removing papers from his briefcase. 'I'll just be a couple of minutes and we can get started.

'Was it the tree branch that kept you, sir?' asked Betts.

'Yes. It came down in last night's storm. It's now lying inside what was once the greenhouse.'

'And the orchids?'

'Well, the hail didn't help, but we saved what we could. And I must give credit to Sophie. She's been a tower of strength over the past twelve hours. I couldn't have done it without her.'

'Don't forget that your neighbour is liable to replace the green-house, sir.'

'I haven't, Betts, but as the rest of the tree fell on to Rhonda Butler's house, I think she has enough to worry about.' Fitzjohn paused. 'She's a pain in the neck is that woman, but I couldn't help but feel sorry for her last night. Her home is decimated. She's lucky to be alive.' Fitzjohn ran his hand over his wispy hair. 'Sophie didn't fair too well either. Not only did she cut her hand on some broken glass, but her mother's ordered her back to Melbourne.'

'I take it she saw Sophie being arrested on the news last night,' said Betts.

'You saw it too, did you?'

'You couldn't miss it, sir. Sophie was on every channel.'

Fitzjohn groaned. 'I'll never hear the end of it from her mother, but I'll see what I can do to get Meg to reverse her decision. After Sophie's valiant efforts to save my orchids, I owe her something. And freedom from her mother's clutches seems to be her highest priority right now.'

Fitzjohn swiveled his chair around to look at the whiteboard. 'Now, enough of my domestic problems. Is there anything I should know before we start this meeting?'

'There is, sir. The man impersonating Pierce Whitehead? His real name is Andrew Braithwaite.'

'*Braithwaite?* Dare I ask if he's related to Phillipa Braithwaite?'

'Her half-brother, sir. Evidently, he has a history of passing himself off in various fields of expertise including architect, airline pilot and civil engineer, to name just a few.' Betts looked back down at his notes. 'Apparently, he built a very impressive bridge in some small African country in 2006.'

'And now he fancies himself as a winemaker,' said Fitzjohn, 'and a good one, according to Rafe Simms.' Fitzjohn chuckled. 'Has he been brought in?'

'About an hour ago, sir. He's also changed his alibi. He now says he spent last Friday night at Phillipa Braithwaite's house. Says he arrived at around 6pm and didn't leave until eight the next morning.'

'Really? I'll be interested to know what changed his mind, and whether Ms Braithwaite agrees with him. We'll speak to her first, Betts,' he added. 'But for now, let's get this meeting underway.'

Fitzjohn and Betts entered The ArtSpace Gallery that afternoon to find Phillipa Braithwaite standing beside a low round table arranging flowers in a vase. She looked over when the door opened.

'Good afternoon, gentlemen,' she said, her hands still clinging to three blue irises.

'Good afternoon, Ms Braithwaite,' said Fitzjohn. 'We'd like to ask you a few more questions, if we may.'

Phillipa placed the remaining irises into the vase and rubbed her hands on a cloth. 'Yes, of course, although I doubt that I can add much to what I told you before, Chief Inspector.' She gave a quick smile and led the way to a group of chairs at the side of the gallery. As she did so, the telephone rang. Phillipa gestured to her assistant. 'Will you get that, Trudy? If it's for me tell them I'll ring them back. Sorry about that, Chief Inspector,' she said as they sat down. 'Have you more questions about Claudia?'

'Not Claudia, Ms Braithwaite. This time we'd like to ask you about Pierce Whitehead.'

'Oh?' Phillipa sat back, crossing her legs. 'Well, all I know about him is that he's the man Claudia employed as her wine-maker at Five Oaks.'

'I see,' said Fitzjohn. 'Well, that surprises me, Ms Braithwaite, because it's come to our attention that Andrew Braithwaite is, in fact, your half-brother.' Phillipa stiffened. 'He tells us he spent last Friday evening - the evening Michael Rossi died - at your home, and didn't leave until eight the following morning. Is that correct?'

'No, it isn't.'

'Are you sure about that, Ms Braithwaite? This is a murder investigation.'

Phillipa Braithwaite bristled. 'I'm well aware of that, Chief Inspector, and I'm quite sure Andrew was not at my home last Friday night. I've had little or nothing to do with my half-brother for a number of years.'

'But surely you had a hand in securing his position as wine-maker at Five Oaks Winery. After all, it would be too much of a coincidence to assume otherwise.'

'Very well. I admit I did introduce Andrew to Claudia when she was looking for a winemaker. And I've regretted the deception ever since.' Phillipa paused. 'Sometimes when family is involved, Chief Inspector, we do things we might otherwise not. My only solace is that I knew he had the ability to do the job. Any job, as it turns out,' she added, her eyebrows rising.

'So we understand,' replied Fitzjohn. 'We will need you to make an official statement refuting your brother's alibi, Ms Braithwaite. And in view of the seriousness of the matter, it'll have to be done immediately.'

Phillipa looked at her watch. 'And I'll do that gladly, Chief Inspector, but I'm afraid it'll have to be later today because I have clients due in less than ten minutes.'

'Alas. This can't wait, Ms Braithwaite, I suggest you have your assistant make other arrangements for your clients.'

———

'So, who do you think is lying, Betts?' said Fitzjohn, sitting back in his chair. 'Andrew Braithwaite or his half-sister, Phillipa.'

'I can't see why Andrew Braithwaite would lie about being at Phillipa's unless he was sure she'd back him up, sir.'

'I agree and I'd say he's going to be surprised to hear she didn't. Let's go and tell him, shall we?'

Fitzjohn and Betts walked into the interview room to find Andrew Braithwaite, alias Pierce Whitehead, sitting next to his solicitor. While Fitzjohn arranged his papers, Betts turned on the recording device and started the formalities, stating the place, time and date. Andrew Braithwaite hesitated before following the others in stating his name.

'So, your name isn't Pierce Whitehead after all, but Andrew Braithwaite,' said Fitzjohn.

Displaying an air of amusement, Braithwaite sat back in his chair. 'Occupational hazard, Chief Inspector. Being sprung, that is.'

'Do you get sprung often?'

'No. I'm usually well away before that happens. But this time was different. I really enjoyed being a winemaker. That's why I stayed on after Claudia died.'

Fitzjohn looked down at his papers. 'Andrew James Braithwaite, half-brother to Phillipa Braithwaite.'

'You have it in one, Chief Inspector. Phillipa was six when my mother married my father, James Braithwaite. I'm not sure Phillipa ever got over having to change her name - to Braithwaite, that is. And yet she's kept it. I've always found that rather curious.'

'I take it Phillipa had a hand in securing your position at Five Oaks Winery,' continued Fitzjohn.

'Of course. What are families for if not to help each other?' Braithwaite chuckled to himself.

'Why did you do it, Mr Braithwaite? And why did you impersonate Pierce Whitehead, in particular?'

'Why not? Pierce and I had studied together some years earlier. I'd heard about his death. It wasn't difficult to persuade Claudia to employ me as her winemaker. After all, Pierce had impeccable credentials.'

'It seems you have quite a history of impersonations, only this time, it's got you mixed up in a murder investigation.' Braithwaite met Fitzjohn's intent gaze.

'I didn't kill Mike Rossi, Chief Inspector. As I told your Sergeant earlier, I was at Phillipa's the night Mike died. If you don't believe me, why don't you ask Phillipa?'

'We have, Mr Braithwaite. She denies you were there on Friday evening.'

The first sign of panic came to Andrew Braithwaite's face. 'The bitch.' Braithwaite ran his hand through his hair. 'Look, I admit Mike and I didn't get on, but I had nothing to do with his death. I swear it.'

'Be that as it may,' replied Fitzjohn, 'we believe you had a strong motive to kill Michael Rossi. After all, he did dismiss you, and without notice. That must have put you in a precarious situation. Not to mention the fact that you're a wanted man. Something to do with passing yourself off as a commercial airline pilot, I believe. It seems you stayed a little too long in that occupation as well.' Fitzjohn sat back with his hands clasped and tapped his thumbs together. 'It doesn't look good, Mr Braithwaite.' Fitzjohn unclasped his hands. 'You'll be held in custody and questioned further, not only about your involvement in Michael Rossi's death, but your escapade as a pilot. However, before that happens, I'd like to question you about Claudia Rossi.'

'Claudia?' Andrew Braithwaite's brow furrowed.

'Yes. Can you tell us the last time you saw Claudia Rossi?'

'It was the week before she died.' Braithwaite cleared his throat. 'I'd come down to Sydney to organise Five Oaks Winery's participation in the Sydney Boutique Wine Fair; I planned to showcase a selection of our wines. I called into Phillipa's afterwards and Claudia happened to be there.'

'And what day of the week was this?' asked Fitzjohn.

'It was a Thursday evening. I remember because I'd made my trip to coincide with Phillipa's return from Melbourne. She'd been there earlier in the week.'

'Melbourne?'

'Yes. She manages an art gallery there. She makes several trips a month.'

'I see,' said Fitzjohn, his interest piqued. 'As a matter of interest, Mr Braithwaite, what was your reason for seeing Phillipa?' Braithwaite fell silent. 'Well?' When he did not reply, Fitzjohn continued. 'Let me remind you, Mr Braithwaite, you're facing serious charges, and not answering our questions isn't going to help you. And it doesn't seem to me that your half-sister intends to either.'

Andrew Braithwaite sighed. 'Mmm. I think you might be right. So much for brotherly love. Okay. I'll tell you what I know, but it doesn't have anything to do with Claudia.'

'We'll make that judgment,' replied Fitzjohn.

'The reason I went to see Phillipa is because she'd asked me to persuade a local artist to sell his work through me.' Andrew Braithwaite looked down at his clasped hands. 'I told him I was an art dealer. It wasn't too difficult to get him to agree.'

'Why didn't Phillipa approach him herself?' asked Fitzjohn.

'She said she had, but without success. Anyway, I called around to Phillipa's to give her the good news.' Braithwaite gave a quick smile.

'And you say that Phillipa had previously tried but failed to obtain any sort of agreement with this artist.'

'Yes. For whatever reason. She didn't offer an explanation.'

'Do you remember the artist's name?'

'No. At the time, it wasn't important to me.'

'In that case, perhaps you can give it some thought while you're being held. Is there anything you'd like to clarify or add before we conclude this interview?' Andrew Braithwaite shook his head. 'Very well, interview terminated at 1640 hours.'

———◦◦◦———

Accompanied by Betts, Fitzjohn walked with a determined gait back to the Incident Room. 'So, according to Andrew Braithwaite, Claudia Rossi was at Phillipa Braithwaite's house on the Thursday evening before she died. And yet, Phillipa Braithwaite denies seeing Claudia at all during that week. One of them is lying, but which one?'

'I'd say it's Phillipa Braithwaite, sir. After all, Andrew Braithwaite isn't aware of the significance of Claudia Rossi being at Phillipa's for dinner during that week.'

'Isn't he? There's always the possibility he is, Betts. Phillipa could have confided in him at some stage. In which case, he's telling us he saw Claudia there that night in retaliation for Phillipa denying his alibi for the night that Michael Rossi died.' Fitzjohn opened the Incident Room door. 'But I don't think that's probable. I agree with you. I think Andrew Braithwaite did see Claudia at Phillipa's that night. And, I suppose you could say that it's understandable that with Claudia dying from mushroom poisoning a couple of days later, Phillipa is reluctant to admit she had her over for dinner. But, where it comes unstuck is in this other matter to do with Phillipa wanting to acquire an agreement with Douglas Porteous. Why didn't she approach Porteous herself?'

'But she did, without success. At least that's what she told Andrew Braithwaite.'

'She's lying, Betts.'

'You mean by having her half-brother make the deal with Porteous, there would be no connection to her.'

'Of course. After all, as far as she knew, no one would ever suspect that Andrew Braithwaite, or Pierce Whitehead as he was known, is her half-brother.' Fitzjohn walked over to his desk. 'Have Mrs Porteous come in to identify Andrew Braithwaite, Betts. If she confirms he's the art dealer who met with Douglas Porteous then we'll speak to Phillipa Braithwaite again.'

'What about Maxwell, sir?'

'Mmm. It's hard to say whether he's involved in the art fraud or not. He might be oblivious to Phillipa's actions. We'll talk to him again, Betts. Have him brought in too, will you. But do it tomorrow. It's been a long day. I want to go home and see what I can do about the tree branch and the remnants of my greenhouse.'

❦ CHAPTER 21 ❧

Betts arrived at Fitzjohn's sandstone cottage in Birchgrove early the next morning, to the sound of a chainsaw. Curious, he made his way along the side of the house and through the gate into the back garden. There, he found Fitzjohn and Sophie, their attention taken by a man sawing through the offending tree branch that now lay ensconced inside the remains of the greenhouse. Betts came to stand next to Fitzjohn. 'This is a lot worse than I imagined,' he shouted over the whining screech. 'There's almost nothing left of the greenhouse.'

'If you think this is bad, take a look at Rhonda Butler's house,' replied Fitzjohn.

Betts cast his eye over the fence. 'My god. The back half of the house has been demolished. And all for a bit of shade. What about Mrs Butler?'

'She's gone to stay with her brother and his wife until it's rebuilt.' Fitzjohn turned back to his greenhouse and Sophie who stood cradling the dusty CD player that had once sat on the shelf just inside the door. He put his arm over Sophie's shoulder and, followed by Betts, they strolled along the garden path to house where rows of orchids huddled together in the shade.

'So, this is what's left,' said Betts, bending down.

'Yes,' said Fitzjohn, sighing.

'I'm just thankful you weren't in the greenhouse when it came down, Uncle Alistair,' said Sophie.

'If you weren't staying with me, Sophie, I probably would have been.' Fitzjohn opened the back door and they walked inside.

'So, my being arrested has had its positive side,' said Sophie, putting the CD player on the kitchen table. 'After all, I wouldn't have been here otherwise.'

'You can't make excuses for getting arrested, Sophie,' replied Fitzjohn, pulling on his suit coat. 'Now remember, I've got those people coming to dismantle what's left of the greenhouse this afternoon. I also want them to scour the garden for pieces of glass.' Fitzjohn picked up his briefcase. 'If you encounter any problems, ring me.'

'I will. And don't worry, Uncle. I'll make sure they take everything away.'

'They're charging enough so see that they do. And I don't want you picking up any more glass,' he added, looking down at Sophie's bandaged hand.

'Now, Betts.' Betts pushed himself away from the side of the kitchen sink. 'I want to speak to Aiden Maxwell this morning. Has he been brought in?'

'Not yet, sir, I thought you might want to look into something else first. Michael Rossi's solicitor, David Spencer, contacted me earlier this morning. He said he'd remembered that Rossi had asked if he could refer him to an Intellectual Property lawyer.'

'When was this?'

'Two weeks ago, sir. Spencer suggested, Magnaut Intellectual Property Law Services. I checked with the firm and apparently, the victim had a consultation with one of their team regarding a patent. Rossi claimed that a patent for one of his own inventions was applied for and given to Robert Nesbit. Since that time the legal firm has set in motion proceedings against Robert Nesbit.'

'That's interesting,' said Fitzjohn, 'because we know Michael Rossi's actions in the past have all but destroyed Nesbit financially, as well as his personal life. This would give Nesbit an even stronger motive to kill Rossi. Okay, Betts. We'll talk to Nesbit this morning instead.'

'It'll have to wait till later this afternoon, sir. I checked with the Cruising Yacht Club. Nesbit's participating in a short ocean race up the coast to Lion Island. They're not due back till at least four this afternoon.'

'Mmm.' Fitzjohn glanced out of the kitchen window at the debris strewn across the back garden. In that case, I'll stay here, for now, and meet you at the yacht club later this afternoon. To be honest, I'd sooner be here when they remove the greenhouse.'

Betts moved toward the door. 'Oh. There's something else you should know. Charlotte Rossi is crewing for Nesbit. Alone.'

Fitzjohn's brow wrinkled. 'I don't like the sound of that, Betts. If Nesbit is the killer he might suspect Charlotte is privy to her uncle's actions against him.'

'Surely he'd realise she wouldn't have gone sailing with him, alone, if she is, sir.'

'If he's just killed a man, Betts, I doubt he's in a stable frame of mind. Anything's possible.'

As the day progressed and with the tree branch and the remnants of the greenhouse gone, Fitzjohn and Sophie stood silently, looking at the empty space. 'It's all a bit of a mess, isn't it, Sophie?'

'Yes, but don't worry, Uncle Alistair, once the new greenhouse is in place, the garden will be restored to its former beauty. You'll see.' Sophie placed a reassuring hand on Fitzjohn's arm. 'I'll even help you to replant all those flowerbeds you've lost.'

'That's good of you, Sophie, but I'm afraid it'll have to wait.' Fitzjohn turned and started to walk back toward the house. 'With my present investigation, I'm in no position to go looking for a new greenhouse.'

'But what about the orchids?' said Sophie, following him. 'They need shelter or they'll die.'

'They won't die, but their condition will deteriorate,' said Fitzjohn gazing down at the rows of orchids lining the back wall of the house. 'Still, it can't be helped.'

Sophie followed Fitzjohn inside. 'I know what we can do, Uncle Alistair. I can see what there is available in greenhouses and gather a few pamphlets together for you. I think I have a fair idea of what you're looking for.'

As Sophie spoke, Fitzjohn's mobile rang. 'Fitzjohn here. No, Betts, I haven't seen the news. I've been outside all day. What's up?' Fitzjohn put his phone on loudspeaker and turned on the television. In silence, he glared at the image of a helicopter hovering above an angry sea where two men were being winched to safety. 'And you say Nesbit's yacht's in trouble?'

'Yes, sir,' replied Betts. 'It was sited outside the Heads not long ago. The mast is broken and Nesbit was unable to get back into the harbour. He's being towed in now by the Water Police.

'I'll meet you at the CYC, Betts. I'm leaving now.'

'There's another problem, sir. Nesbit radioed that Charlotte Rossi went overboard. They're searching for her.' Fitzjohn winced.

Heavy cloud covered the sky and a cool southerly blew as Fitzjohn arrived by taxi at the Cruising Yacht Club. Betts met him at the curb, and they made their way into the club. They found Robert Nesbit's storm battered yacht moored in the marina. Its mast lay across the deck, the remnants of sails strewn about. Nesbit stood in the midst of the chaos. 'Mr Nesbit,' Fitzjohn called. Nesbit, turned, his anguished face one of exhaustion and shock. 'We understand you've been through an ordeal today. Are you able to answer a few questions?' Robert Nesbit did not reply but joined Fitzjohn and Betts on the pontoon. 'We're told Charlotte Rossi was sailing with you, sir.'

'Yes.' Nesbit's face contorted as if reliving the grim reality. 'I feel so responsible. The weather report last night had predicted unsettled weather, but I decided to sail anyway.' He shook his head, his eyes glistening.

'Can you tell us what happened?' asked Fitzjohn.

'I don't see what this has to do with your investigation into Michael Rossi's death, Chief Inspector, but if you insist.' Nesbit ran his hand across the back of his neck. 'The day started out fine and clear, but when we were off Long Reef, a strong southerly started to blow and with it came the storm.' Nesbit swallowed hard. 'I was sure we'd make it back, but the storm moved too fast. Charlotte had just come back up on deck when it happened. She'd gone below to put her wet weather gear on. A wave caught her before she had time to put her safety harness on. She was gone in a second.' Nesbit's voice quivered. 'There was nothing I could do. She disappeared so quickly. It was then I radioed for help.' Nesbit steadied himself on one of the pontoon supports. 'Now if that's all...' he barked at Fitzjohn.

'For the present, Mr Nesbit.' Fitzjohn watched Nesbit climb back on to his yacht and disappear below.

Fitzjohn and Betts retreated along the pontoon. 'I want Robert Nesbit put under surveillance until Charlotte Rossi is found, Betts.'

'And if she isn't, sir?'

'Let's pray to God that she is, Betts. Let's pray to God that she is.'

❧CHAPTER 22❧

E sme, her knuckles white as she gripped the arm of her chair, stared at the images that flashed across the television screen. Images of a dark stormy sea and a man dangling precariously from a helicopter as it hovered above the grey heaving waves. 'You're out there, Charlotte. Somewhere,' she whispered.

Getting to her feet, Esme glanced at the photographs nestled on the table in the corner of the room. Claudia's smiling face, and Michael's. She ran her index finger across the top of the frame that held Thomas's image, his face full of youth. And beside them, another face. Charlotte on her graduation day. Tears came to Esme's eyes. 'Please don't let Charlotte be gone too,' she whispered.

A shiver went through Esme as she walked across to the window to draw the curtains against the growing darkness. It was then she saw the taxi pull up in front of the house and Chief Inspector Fitzjohn get out. News at last, perhaps, she thought. But would it be good news? Esme collected herself, walked out of the living room and turned on the porch light before she opened the front door.

'Chief Inspector. I'm so glad you've come. Or am I?' Esme hesitated. 'Charlotte's one of those lost, isn't she?'

Fitzjohn stepped inside.

'Yes. I'm afraid she is, Miss Timmons.'

Esme shook her head. 'I think I knew,' she said, closing the door behind him. 'Have they found her? Is that why you're here?'

'No. There's been no word yet. I just came to assure you that everything is being done to find your niece, Miss Timmons.'

'I'm sure it is, Chief Inspector. And I appreciate you coming to tell me personally. I've been watching the news all afternoon. I did make a few phone calls, but that didn't get me anywhere.' Esme sighed and took Fitzjohn's arm as they walked together into the living room. 'I watched the weather forecast for the east coast last night, and it didn't look good.' Esme sat in her chair. 'Rafe Simms saw it too. He rang earlier this evening. He got worried when he wasn't able to reach Charlotte on her mobile phone. He knows she sails on weekends, you see.' Esme's fingers followed the intricate pattern of the lace doily on the arm of her chair. 'He and Charlotte were to be married at one time, but the wedding was called off. I don't know why. Charlotte never said. I've always thought it a shame because they are two such wonderful young people.' Esme patted the arm of her chair. 'Anyway, I must telephone Rafe now and tell him that Charlotte is one of those lost at sea.' Esme sighed. 'After I've spoken to him, we'll have some tea. I need to keep myself busy.' She eyed Fitzjohn. 'But there's another reason you're here, isn't there? I can see it in your face. What is it?'

'You're very perceptive, Miss Timmons. And you're right. There is. It's about Robert Nesbit. I understand Charlotte was crewing for him today.'

'Yes, she is. She does most weekends. Is Robert lost too?'

'No. He and his yacht have been towed back into the harbour.'

'Then what is it about him?'

'We've reason to believe he may be involved in your nephew's death, Miss Timmons.' Esme gasped. 'I don't want to alarm you unnecessarily, but...'

'But you think that could be the reason Charlotte went overboard. Oh, dear.'

As the hours passed without word of Charlotte, Esme and Fitzjohn spoke of many things, not the least of which Fitzjohn's late wife, Edith, and the orchids she had left in his care. Esme spoke of her fiancé, Thomas, and their short time together. At 11pm, the sound of Fitzjohn's mobile phone shook them both.

Esme tried to read the countenance of Fitzjohn's face as he spoke. 'Is there news of Charlotte?' she asked as he hung up.

'Yes. She was picked up by a fishing trawler about 20 minutes ago, Miss Timmons. She's being transported by helicopter to St Vincent's Hospital.'

'And her condition?'

'Only that she's unconscious.'

'Well, at least she's alive.'

Esme sat alone in the hospital waiting room near the Intensive Care Unit, the hours ticking by with no word that Charlotte had regained consciousness. Weary, she dozed intermittently, only to be aroused by the medical staff as they worked through the night. It was during one of her wakeful moments, in the dead of night, that the door opened and Rafe Simms appeared.

'How is she, Esme?' he asked, sitting down next to her.

'Not good, I'm afraid,' replied Esme. 'She hasn't regained consciousness.' Esme looked into Rafe's face. 'I won't pretend I'm not worried. It's been hours since they brought her in.' Rafe took Esme's hand.

'I'm so very glad you're here,' she said.

❦CHAPTER 23❧

With the enormity of the previous twelve hours, Fitzjohn returned home in the early hours of Sunday morning to change before making his way to Kings Cross Police Station. He met up with Betts in the corridor. 'Any word on Charlotte Rossi, Betts?'

'Not yet, sir.'

Fitzjohn looked at his watch. 'It's been almost 12 hours since they found her,' he said, his eyebrows knitting together. 'Doesn't look good, does it?' They walked into the Incident Room where Fitzjohn put his briefcase on his desk and sat down. 'We'll wait for news of Ms Rossi before we speak to Robert Nesbit again. In the meantime, I want to interview Aiden Maxwell. I take it he's been brought in.'

'Yes, sir. He's waiting in one of the interview rooms. But before we do, sir, the results are back from forensics on Miss Timmons's walking cane. They found traces of hair and blood.'

Fitzjohn sat back and half smiled. 'So, Miss Timmons hit her target after all. Now we just have to find out who it was.'

'There's something else, sir. Graeme Wyngard, the owner of the yacht Michael Rossi's body fell from, has brought in a lipstick he says doesn't belong to either his wife or his two daughters.'

'A previous owner of the yacht, perhaps?' suggested Fitzjohn.

Betts shook his head. 'Mr Wyngard says not, sir. He says he purchased the yacht two weeks ago and only took possession of it three days before Michael Rossi's death. He's adamant that the only women who've been on the yacht are his wife and daughters.'

'I see. In that case, it could turn up something. I hope it does because we don't seem to be getting anywhere at the moment.' Fitzjohn gathered his papers together. 'Let's see what Maxwell has to say.'

Aiden Maxwell sat alone at the table in the interview room. Impeccably dressed in a light grey, double-breasted suit with electric blue bow tie and matching breast pocket handkerchief, he looked the embodiment of good fashion. 'Good morning, Mr Maxwell.' Fitzjohn and Betts took their seats. 'You don't choose to have counsel?' asked Fitzjohn, looking at Maxwell over the top of his glasses.

'I can't see why I should need a solicitor, Chief Inspector.'

'As you wish.' Fitzjohn placed his papers on the desk in front of him. 'If you change your mind during the interview, please let us know.' Fitzjohn nodded to Betts who switched on the recording device and after going through the formalities, the interview began. 'Now, Mr Maxwell, I'd like to start by asking you further questions about Claudia Rossi.'

'But I've already told you all I know,' answered Maxwell, his voice rising in intensity.

Fitzjohn smiled. 'These are different questions.' Maxwell looked to brace himself. Noticing this Fitzjohn asked again, 'Are you sure you wouldn't like a solicitor present?'

'Quite sure, thank you.' Maxwell clasped his hands together on the desk.

'Very well. I understand that in June 2010, you sold a Brandt sketch to Claudia Rossi for the sum of $150,000.'

'I'd have to check my records for the exact price but, yes, I did sell that piece of art work to Claudia.'

'Can you tell us how you came by the sketch, Mr Maxwell?'

'Phillipa Braithwaite procured it. It's part of her position in my employ. She does most of the buying. I used to do it myself, but she's gradually taken over that role. I'm sure Ms Braithwaite will be able to help you there.'

'So there'll be details of that particular purchase kept on file, I assume?'

'Yes, of course. Phillipa keeps all those records at the gallery in Mosman.' Maxwell's brow wrinkled. 'Can I ask why you're asking about the sketch?'

'Because the Brandt sketch is a fake, Mr Maxwell."

'I *beg* your pardon.'

'Just what I said,' replied Fitzjohn. 'We've had the sketch examined by an expert who has deemed it not authentic.'

Aiden Maxwell stared at Fitzjohn his face a mixture of anguish and confusion. He slumped back in his chair. 'I don't know what to say. This is not only shocking, but embarrassing...' Maxwell ran his trembling hand through his hair. 'I've always prided myself in my expertise. Are you absolutely sure about this, Chief Inspector?'

'Quite sure, Mr Maxwell.'

'And you think I had something to do with it?' Maxwell raised his eyes to the ceiling.

'That's not necessarily the case,' said Fitzjohn, 'but I must alert you to the fact that we are investigating Claudia Rossi's death, so if you do know anything, however insignificant you might think it is, it would be in your best interest to tell us.'

'But I told you everything I know the last time we spoke.'

'And I seem to remember you said Claudia Rossi came to see you about the provenance of a piece of art work that had been purchased by the New South Wales Art Gallery.'

'That's right. She did.'

'And she didn't talk to you about the provenance of the Brandt sketch at that time?'

'No. I wouldn't forget something like that. In fact, if she had asked me about the sketch it would have alerted me to the fact that there was something wrong.'

'So, what you're saying is that Claudia Rossi at no time spoke to you about the sketch, and you had no idea that it's a fake.' Fitzjohn waited for Maxwell to reply. 'Is that correct?'

'Yes. Yes, it is.'

'Are you sure, Mr Maxwell? The reason I ask is because we're led to believe that Claudia Rossi's daughter, Charlotte Rossi, approached you only the other day regarding the Brandt sketch's provenance. We also understand that you offered to look into the matter for her.' Fitzjohn glared at Aiden Maxwell. 'Well?'

Maxwell cleared his throat. 'All right. Claudia did ask me about the sketch's provenance, and so did her daughter, Charlotte.'

'Then why did you lie to us?' asked Fitzjohn.

'Because my reputation's at stake here, Chief Inspector. A breath of scandal and I'll be ruined!'

'Lying to the police isn't going to help keep you from ruin, Mr Maxwell.' Fitzjohn turned over to the next sheet of paper that lay on the table in front of him. 'Let's go back to Claudia Rossi. When did you last see her?'

'It was on that Sunday I told you about the last time we spoke,' replied Maxwell, his voice trembling. 'We had planned to meet again on the following Thursday evening - Claudia wanted to return a painting she'd restored for me - but I had to cancel because I needed to go to Melbourne. I like to visit my mother a couple of times each month. Since she lost my father, she gets quite lonely.'

Fitzjohn glimpsed another side to Aiden Maxwell, or was it another lie? 'When did you get back from Melbourne, Mr Maxwell?'

'The following Sunday. The day after Claudia died.'

'Check out Maxwell's alibi for the week Claudia died, Betts,' said Fitzjohn as they made their way back to the Incident Room. See if he was in Melbourne visiting his mother that week.' Fitzjohn threw his papers on to his desk and sat down heavily in his chair before removing his glasses. 'Let's go through what we have so far on Claudia Rossi.'

Betts sat down at his desk and opened his notebook. 'For a start,' he began, 'we know that Claudia met with Aiden Maxwell on Sunday, July 11, 2010. Six days before her death. We also know she spent a few days during that week at the National Art Gallery in Canberra, returning to Sydney on Thursday, July 15. Andrew Braithwaite tells us that the last time he saw Claudia was at Phillipa Braithwaite's home on that Thursday evening. On Friday, July 16th, Claudia's daughter, Charlotte arrived from Adelaide around lunch time and stayed until, approximately, seven-thirty the following morning. Claudia was admitted to hospital later that morning.'

'And what about the mushrooms,' asked Fitzjohn. 'According to the Coroner's report, Claudia could have picked them in Canberra and brought them back to Sydney herself. Andrew Braithwaite tells us that his half-sister, Phillipa, spent the earlier part of that week in Melbourne where such mushrooms are to be found. And Charlotte Rossi returned from Adelaide on semester break where it's also possible to find death cap mushrooms.'

'And then there's the Brandt sketch, and the way in which it was purchased by Maxwell's galleries.' said Fitzjohn.

'Well,' replied Betts, 'according to Maxwell, Phillipa Braithwaite does all the buying for his galleries and he appears to have little or no knowledge of the way in which the sketch was procured. Furthermore, he appeared to be oblivious to the fact that the sketch is a fake, and denied being asked about its provenance. Until, of course, you confronted him, and he admitted that both Claudia and Charlotte had approached him about its provenance.'

'And last but not least,' said Fitzjohn, 'there's Andrew Braithwaite who admits to posing as an art dealer at the behest of Phillipa so that she could engage Porteous as one of her suppliers of art. Get a search warrant from the Magistrate for The ArtSpace Gallery and Phillipa Braithwaite's home, Betts.'

'What are we looking for, sir?'

'All records pertaining to the purchase of art work for all Maxwell's galleries, in particular, the record of the Brandt sketches procurement. We'll do the searches simultaneously. Shouldn't be too difficult to find the purchase order if it does exist.'

'Any news on Charlotte Rossi yet?'

'No, sir.'

———⟶⟐⟵———

Fitzjohn, along with Betts and Williams, arrived at Phillipa Braithwaite's home early the following morning. The front door opened as Fitzjohn put his hand up to knock and Phillipa Braithwaite appeared. Fitzjohn smiled. 'I take it you're on your way out, Ms Braithwaite.'

Phillipa grappled with her handbag and briefcase in the face of the three officers. 'I'm on my way to work, Chief Inspector. I have an early appointment with a client.'

'Then we'll try not to keep you too long. We have search warrants for both your home and The ArtSpace Gallery. Our officers are at the gallery as we speak. This is the warrant to search these premises.' Fitzjohn handed Phillipa Braithwaite the warrant.

'For heaven's sake,' she said, her eyes scanning the document. 'What are you looking for?'

'As you can see, we're here to seize all records pertaining to the procurement of art work by the three galleries owned by Aiden Maxwell. We understand you are the principle buyer.'

'I am, but you didn't need search warrants to view the files. You only needed to ask. And I don't keep any files at home. They're in my office at the Mosman gallery.'

'Nevertheless, Ms Braithwaite, to satisfy the requirements of our investigation, we *will* search your premises.' Fitzjohn moved forward and Phillipa backed into the house, its paintings and oriental rugs imparting a tone of sophistication and wealth.

'This is preposterous,' said Phillipa, entering the living room and setting her briefcase, and her handbag, on the sofa.

'That remains to be seen,' said Fitzjohn. 'Now why don't you and I sit in here while my officers conduct their search?' Glaring at Fitzjohn, Phillipa sat down on the sofa and folded her arms while Fitzjohn settled himself into an armchair. In the strained atmosphere, he took in the room, its traditional furniture lending an air of comfort, despite its classic style. His eyes moved from the assortment of art books on the table next to him, to the antique clock on the mantelpiece below a gilt framed mirror, before they came to rest on an object in the Edwardian china cabinet. Getting to his feet, he strolled around the room, nonchalantly peering at various pictures before passing in front of the china cabinet.

'You have a fine collection of paintings, Ms Braithwaite,' he said sitting down again. Phillipa shrugged and the strained atmosphere continued until Betts and Williams appeared with a laptop and two boxes of files.

'We found these, sir,' said Betts in a low voice.

Phillipa Braithwaite sneered. 'You'll find nothing in there. That's my personal filing.'

'In that case, Ms Braithwaite, it will be returned to you intact after we're finished with it,' said Fitzjohn. 'Good day to you.' With that, Fitzjohn followed Betts and Williams from the house.'

'I can't say what we have here, sir,' said Betts. 'Could amount to nothing.'

'Even if it does, Betts, I believe, our search wasn't in vain. I want you to obtain another warrant for Phillipa Braithwaite's home.'

Betts looked at Fitzjohn in disbelief. 'But...'

'This time in search of a Limoges perfume bottle.' Fitzjohn gave a wry smile. 'You'll find it in the china cabinet amongst the figurines.'

❊{CHAPTER 24}❊

Fitzjohn sat alone in the Incident Room turning his pen end for end. He threw it down when the door opened and Betts walked in. 'By the look on your face, Betts, I'd say we're in business.'

'We are, sir. A purchase order for the Brandt sketch was found amongst the files we seized from Phillipa Braithwaite's home. It's made out to someone by the name of Wesley Hammond. We approached the taxation office and they've conducted enquiries on our behalf.'

'And?' prompted Fitzjohn.

'The enquiries lead us to believe that Wesley Hammond doesn't exist.'

'Just as I thought.' Fitzjohn got to his feet and started to pull his suit coat on. 'What about the perfume bottle?'

'It was where you said it would be, sir. In the china cabinet. Miss Timmons has confirmed that it's the one missing from her home since the night of Michael Rossi's death. I've had Phillipa

Braithwaite brought in for questioning. She's waiting in one of the interview rooms.'

A satisfied look came to Fitzjohn's face.

'There's something else you should know before you question her, sir. Trudy James, Phillipa Braithwaite's assistant has come forward. She said that Michael Rossi came to the gallery to speak to Phillipa Braithwaite a little after 4pm on the day that he died. She said she doesn't know what they spoke about, but she did hear raised voices coming from Phillipa's office.'

'Why on earth didn't she come forward with this information before?' said Fitzjohn, an exasperated look on his face.

'She says she didn't think it important at the time, although I suspect it might have something to do with loyalty to her employer. I imagine she changed her mind when the police arrived with the search warrant.'

Fitzjohn shook his head. 'Very well. Another piece of the puzzle into Rossi's whereabouts before he died. He must have gone to the gallery straight after speaking to Richard Edwards at the hospital, and before he paid a call to the New South Wales Art Gallery.' Fitzjohn sat in thought for a moment. 'So, Phillipa Braithwaite knew all along that he was back in Sydney on that Friday.'

Phillipa Braithwaite was found pacing the floor when, a few minutes later, Fitzjohn and Betts entered the interview room. Her solicitor looked up from his notes when they appeared. Phillipa pulled out a chair and sat down, her indignation apparent. 'It's about time,' she said, icily. 'Do you realise I've been kept waiting for over an hour?'

'Our apologies, Ms Braithwaite,' said Fitzjohn. 'Unfortunately, the cogs in the wheel don't always move as fast as we would like.' He half smiled and sat down.

'Unfortunate isn't the word,' Phillipa continued. 'Your tardiness has cost me a very important sale.'

'That's neither here nor there to me, Ms Braithwaite,' answered Fitzjohn. 'I'm investigating two murders and in so doing, I have a number of questions to put to you. Firstly, I want to know how you came by the Limoges perfume bottle found at your place of residence in Double Bay.' Phillipa did not reply. 'We know it was stolen from Esme Timmons's home at approximately 2:23am on the morning of Saturday, March 18th. We also have a sworn statement from your half-brother, Andrew Braithwaite, that you were absent from your home between 1am and 3:30am on that morning.' Fitzjohn waited for Phillipa Braithwaite to respond. 'Of course, you're not obliged to answer my questions, but I should advise you that it could work against your best interests if you don't.'

Phillipa sat still, avoiding Fitzjohn's gaze. Finally, she turned to her solicitor and whispered in his ear. After his reply she said, 'All right. I did go to Esme's that night and I did take the perfume bottle.'

'But that wasn't your reason for going, was it, Ms Braithwaite? It was to recover these.' Fitzjohn placed three plastic sheaves on the table. 'Three letters sent to Claudia Rossi, describing her partner's infidelity. Anonymous letters.' Phillipa Braithwaite glared at the letters. 'Your handiwork.'

'He used me,' Phillipa said at last.

'Who used you, Ms Braithwaite?'

'Richard.'

'Richard Edwards?' ask Fitzjohn.

'Yes.' The room filled with Phillipa's curdled laughter. 'He thought he could walk away from me just like that. I was doing Claudia a favour. She needed to know what a cretin she was living with.'

'So what made you think these letters would be in the study in Esme Timmons's home?'

'Because the study is where Claudia kept all her personal papers, and it was where she'd showed me the first letter she'd received.' Phillipa chuckled to herself. 'She had no idea. No idea at all that I'd sent it.'

'But why did you choose that particular night to break into Esme Timmons's home? Why hadn't you tried to get the letters back before?' Phillipa did not reply. 'Was it because Michael Rossi came to see you on the Friday afternoon before his death? After Richard Edwards told him that you were the woman he'd had an affair with, and that you'd sent those poison pen letters to Claudia?' Phillipa continued her silence. 'Might you also have been looking for a report that Claudia Rossi had been compiling on the provenance of the Brandt sketch, Ms Braithwaite?'

'No. Why would I want that?'

'I can think of a number of reasons. Firstly, according to the purchase order that was seized from your home, you bought that sketch from a man by the name of Wesley Hammond.' Fitzjohn handed Phillipa a copy of the purchase order.

'If that's what the purchase order says,' answered Phillipa, barely looking at it. 'I do a lot of buying, Chief Inspector. I don't remember names.'

'So, as far as you're concerned, Wesley Hammond is the person you bought the Brandt sketch from.'

'Yes.'

'Then that does surprise me, Ms Braithwaite, because Wesley Hammond doesn't exist.' Fitzjohn sat back in his chair. 'Not only does he not exist, but we've also discovered that the Brandt sketch is a fake, painted by an artist by the name of Douglas Porteous.' Fitzjohn's eyes locked onto Phillipa. 'Does the name ring any bells? He's the man you had your half-brother, Andrew Braithwaite, approach in order to buy the sketch, isn't he?' Phillipa sank back in her chair. 'You said earlier that you didn't see Claudia Rossi during the week before she died, and yet we have a witness who attests to the fact that you did. In fact, Claudia came to your home for dinner on Thursday, July 15, 2010.'

'Let me guess. Andrew told you that.' Phillipa sighed. 'All right. Claudia was at my home that night for dinner, but I didn't...'

'Didn't what, Ms Braithwaite?'

'I didn't cook the meal.'

'Then who did?'

'It was Aiden. Claudia had been to see him the previous Sunday. About the sketch. He could see she was going to find out about the art fraud and he panicked. His reputation is everything to him. He insisted I invite Claudia over for dinner that Thursday night. I swear I didn't know what he was planning to do. He just said we had to convince her that the sketch wasn't a fake.' Phillipa paused. 'It wasn't unusual for the three of us to dine together, or for Aiden to prepare the meal. We dined together quite often.'

'So, what are you saying?' asked Fitzjohn. 'That Aiden Maxwell served the poisonous mushrooms to Claudia that evening at dinner?'

'Yes.' Phillipa paused. 'I found out later that he'd brought them back from Melbourne the day before.'

'Why didn't you go to the police, Ms Braithwaite?'

'Because Aiden said I'd not only be implicated in Claudia's death, but also the sale of the fake Brandt sketch.'

Fitzjohn set his pen down carefully on the papers in front of him. 'To be quite honest, Ms Braithwaite, I can't see how he could have brought death cap mushrooms back from Melbourne the day before because Aiden Maxwell was still in Melbourne on July the 14th, 2010. In fact, he'd left for Melbourne after his meeting with Claudia on Sunday, July 11th and didn't return to Sydney until the following Sunday, the 17th. The day after Claudia Rossi died.' Phillipa opened her mouth to speak as Betts cautioned her.

'Phillipa Braithwaite, I'm arresting you for the murder of Claudia Rossi...'

Fitzjohn sat back in his chair that afternoon, a satisfied look on his face. 'It's been a worthwhile day, Betts. Not only were we able to establish that it was Phillipa Braithwaite who committed the home invasion at Esme Timmons house, but she also admitted to writing those three anonymous letters to Claudia Rossi. Not to mention employing Andrew Braithwaite to act as an art dealer in order to procure Douglas Porteous's work.' Fitzjohn paused. 'Now all we have to do is find Michael Rossi's killer.' Fitzjohn turned as the Incident Room door opened and Reynolds appeared.

'Any news, Reynolds?' he asked.

'Yes, sir. Eunice Porteous has identified Andrew Braithwaite as the art dealer her husband dealt with.'

'Excellent.'

'And Charlotte Rossi has regained consciousness, sir.'

'Thank heaven for that.' Fitzjohn brought his chair forward. 'Were you able to speak to her, Reynolds?'

'Only for a minute or two, but enough time to find out that Robert Nesbit didn't have anything to do with her going overboard in that storm. In fact, she said he tried everything he could to reach her.'

'I see. Did she say why she wasn't wearing a safety harness?'

'Apparently, she'd taken it off to go below to put on her wet weather gear, sir. When she came back on deck a wave caught her before she could put the safety harness back on.'

'So, Robert Nesbit was telling the truth.' Fitzjohn thought for a moment. 'But it doesn't change the fact that he's our main person of interest into Michael Rossi's death.' He looked over to Reynolds. 'Impound Nesbit's yacht, Reynolds, and have him brought in for questioning.' Fitzjohn responded to Betts's enquiring look. 'There's something Nesbit's not telling us, Betts. I feel it in my bones.'

Accompanied by Betts, Fitzjohn entered the interview room where Robert Nesbit sat with his solicitor. Betts turned on the recording device and went through the preliminaries. Nesbit watched with an indignant expression. 'Why have I been brought here, Chief Inspector? If you think I had anything to do with Charlotte going into the sea, you're mistaken.'

'This is nothing to do with Charlotte Rossi, Mr Nesbit,' said Fitzjohn. 'Ms Rossi has confirmed that the incident on your yacht was an accident. No. We wish to talk to you about an entirely different matter. A patent, in fact.' Nesbit drew himself up in his chair. 'We understand that shortly after Michael Rossi left the company that you and he, along with Richard Edwards, partnered, you applied for a patent for a yachting device you claim to have invented. Is that true?'

'Yes. What of it?'

Fitzjohn ignored Nesbit's retort. 'We also understand that Michael Rossi claimed he was, in fact, the inventor of that device and last week approached an intellectual property law firm providing them with evidence in support of his claim. Further to that, Mr Rossi gave them instructions to take up a case against you, We're also led to believe that that law firm wrote to you concerning this matter, advising that if you didn't withdraw the application forthwith, legal proceedings would be initiated against you.'

Nesbit ran his hand inside his shirt collar. 'I deserve that patent if for nothing else than payment for what Mike put me through.'

'So you concede it was Michael Rossi's invention.'

'Look, the man ruined my life.' Nesbit threw his hands in the air. 'My marriage, the business. Everything. But I didn't kill him.' Nesbit glared at Fitzjohn.

'Why should we believe you, Mr Nesbit? After all, you did have a strong motive.'

'As I told you before, I was at the hospital on the Friday evening Mike died.' Nesbit fiddled with his watchband. 'The nursing staff can verify that.'

'You were at the hospital for some of that evening, yes,' said Fitzjohn, 'but not, unfortunately for you, during the time of Michael Rossi's death.'

Nesbit swallowed hard under Fitzjohn's intense gaze. 'All right. I did leave the hospital for a short time because I wanted to speak to Mike. About the patent. I'd tried when we'd met earlier that evening at the CYC, but Mike seemed preoccupied. I arrived to find his office open but Mike wasn't there. I knew he was around because his briefcase was on the cupboard behind his desk, and the desk lamp was on. I figured he must have gone down to the marina, so I walked out on to the balcony outside his office to see if I could see him.'

'And did you?'

'At the time I thought I did, but since...'

'Go on.'

'There were two people on the deck of one of the yachts.'

'Where exactly was this yacht moored, Mr Nesbit?'

'It was directly below the balcony. The two people on board had their backs to me. A man and a woman. As I said, I thought the man was Mike. It wasn't until the next morning that I realised what I might have witnessed.'

'What do you mean?'

Nesbit hesitated. 'While I stood there, they pushed something into the water. I heard the splash. I didn't think much about it at the time. I thought it was probably a fender.' He looked at Fitzjohn. 'It protects the top side of the yacht. Anyway, when I heard the news about Mike's death the next morning...'

'Do you have any thoughts about who these two people were, Mr Nesbit?'

'No. It was too dark to see them that well.'

'Can you think of anything, anything at all about these two people, Mr Nesbit? For instance, were they tall, short, fat, thin?' Nesbit thought for a moment.

'Well, put like that, the woman was fairly tall. And slim. The man was of medium height and build. Like Mike. That's why I'd thought it was him at first.'

'Why didn't you come forward with this information, Mr Nesbit?'

'Because I didn't want to get involved, Chief Inspector. Not with Mike and me having our differences.'

'But you're involved now anyway, aren't you?' Fitzjohn scratched the back of his neck.

<hr>

'How did you know that Nesbit wasn't at the hospital at the time of Michael Rossi's death,' asked Betts as they left the interview room.

'I didn't,' replied Fitzjohn, grinning.

'Do you belief what he said about these two people being on the yacht that night, sir?'

'Do you, Betts?'

'It's hard to say, sir.'

'In that case,' said Fitzjohn, 'let's suppose that Robert Nesbit is telling the truth. So, we're looking for a tall, slim, female, and a man of medium build. Not a lot to go on, but who do we know who fit those descriptions?'

'Phillipa Braithwaite and her half-brother, Andrew,' offered Betts. 'And Charlotte Rossi, although I wouldn't call Ms Rossi particularly tall.'

'What about Stella Rossi and Nigel Prentice?' asked Fitzjohn. 'They both match those descriptions, and we know they spent the evening together. We'll start by speaking to Stella Rossi. Have her brought in, Betts.'

'What shall I do with Robert Nesbit, sir?'

'Keep him here for now.'

{CHAPTER 25}

The strange world of shadows and muffled sounds that surrounded Charlotte faded and, once again, she gasped for air as she struggled to keep her face above the surface of the heaving sea. Fighting against the wind as it whipped across the top of the waves, its stinging spray blotting her vision, a sense of dread took hold when she could no longer see the yacht. She struggled to stay afloat, but as her body grew cold, her panic subsided and a tranquil feeling of which she had never felt before, ensued as Charlotte slowly sank. But there they were again, the muffled sounds, robbing her of the peace she sought. Was that Rafe's voice?

'Charlotte? Can you hear me?'

Charlotte's eyes fluttered before focusing on Esme who sat at her bedside. 'Esme? Where am I?'

'You're in St Vincent's Hospital, dear.' Esme gently rubbed Charlotte's hand. 'Do you remember what happened when you were sailing?'

'I was in the water. I couldn't... breath.' A tremor went through Charlotte as the memory surfaced. 'The storm... Where's Robert?'

'Robert made it back into Sydney Harbour with help from the Water Police. He's fine. Now you must rest. You've been through a terrible ordeal.' Esme patted Charlotte's hand. 'I'm so thankful you're back at last.'

'I thought I heard Rafe's voice.'

'You did. He's been at your bedside for the past 48 hours,' said Esme, smiling. 'He just stepped out for a minute or two.' As Esme spoke, the door opened and the tall figure of Rafe Simms walked into the room.

'Here he is now,' said Esme. Esme got to her feet as Rafe reached the bedside. 'I'll leave you two for now. I finally feel like having a bite to eat. Thank God you're back with us, Charlotte, dear.' Esme patted Rafe's arm. 'Look after her, Rafe.'

Rafe sat down as Esme left the room. Neither he nor Charlotte spoke for a few moments. 'Thanks for being here, Rafe,' Charlotte said at last.

'I wouldn't wish to be anywhere else. I lost you once. I don't plan on that happening again.' Rafe smiled. 'I can see that I'm going to have to keep closer tabs on you.'

Charlotte's thoughts went to Sally. 'Sally might not appreciate that.'

'Sally's working holiday came to an end shortly after you came to Five Oaks that day. She's gone back to the UK.'

❦CHAPTER 26❧

S
tella Rossi, her face drawn and pale, sat quietly beside her solicitor as Fitzjohn and Betts entered the interview room. 'Surely you could have spoken to me at home, Chief Inspector,' she said in a quiet voice as Fitzjohn sat down. 'Being brought here with my solicitor, not to mention being finger printed is very distressing.'

'Nevertheless, Mrs Rossi,' replied Fitzjohn, 'we found it necessary to conduct this interview here at the station so that it can be recorded.' Fitzjohn sat down and, at the same time, nodded to Betts who commenced the preliminaries. After those present had announced themselves, he continued. 'I'd like to start, Mrs Rossi, by asking you where you were between the hours of seven and midnight on Friday, March 17th.'

'I've already told you that.'

'We want it recorded, Mrs Rossi,' replied Fitzjohn.

Stella sighed. 'All right. I was at a function at the art gallery with my friend, Janet Gibson. Who, I might add, has confirmed that fact.'

'So she has,' said Fitzjohn, looking down at the papers in front of him. 'And what did you do after the function?'

'You know that too. I went for a drive with Nigel Prentice.'

'Where to?'

'We drove up to Colloroy.'

'And can you tell us where exactly you stopped the car?'

'At the beach. We parked at the beach,' said Stella with growing agitation.

'How long were you there, Mrs Rossi?'

'Oh. Look. This is ridiculous. *I don't know.* At the time, I wasn't looking at my watch.' Stella leant over to her solicitor.

'My client doesn't wish to answer any more questions, Chief Inspector.' At that moment, the door opened and Williams came into the interview room and whispered in Fitzjohn's ear. Fitzjohn turned to Stella Rossi's solicitor.

'We'll terminate the interview and resume in half an hour at which time I'll have more questions for your client.' The solicitor nodded.

'She's becoming agitated, sir,' said Betts as he and Fitzjohn followed Williams to the Incident Room.

'Mmm. There might be more to Stella Rossi than we first thought, Betts.'

Once in the Incident Room, Fitzjohn turned to Williams. 'What is it, Williams?'

'The report on the lipstick found on Mr Wyngard's yacht has come back from forensics, sir. With their findings, I thought you'd want to know before you continue interviewing Stella Rossi. There was a clear fingerprint on the case, and another, not as clear, on the velvet cover. They've been matched with those of Stella Rossi.'

'Which puts her on that yacht.' Fitzjohn turned to Betts. 'Remind me, Betts. How long had the yacht been at the marina for alterations?'

Betts looked in his notebook. 'It arrived around 5pm on Friday, March 17th, sir.'

'So, if what Graeme Wyngard says is accurate, and that lipstick doesn't belong to any female members of his family, it must have been left on the yacht after 5pm on the night Michael Rossi died.' Fitzjohn looked back at Williams. 'Sergeant, keeping in mind the continuity of evidence, arrange for me to take the lipstick into our interview with Stella Rossi.'

Fitzjohn and Betts re-entered the interview room to find Stella Rossi in conversation with her solicitor. They stopped talking when the door opened and the solicitor addressed Fitzjohn.

'My client has changed her mind, Chief Inspector, she now wishes to continue with the interview.'

After going through the preliminaries again, Fitzjohn continued. 'Mrs Rossi, you've stated that on the night of Friday, March 17th, you spent the evening with Nigel Prentice at Colloroy, and you didn't return home until almost midnight.'

'That's right.'

Fitzjohn eyed Stella Rossi as he placed the plastic bag containing the lipstick in front of her. 'Do you recognise this?' he asked. 'A Sisley brand lipstick. Made in Paris.'

'I've never used that brand.'

'That surprises me, Mrs Rossi, because your fingerprints have been found on the case and the velvet cover.' Stella Rossi stiffened. 'I should also inform you that this lipstick was found on the yacht from which Michael Rossi fell on the night in question. A yacht that had only been at the marina since 5pm that afternoon.' Fitzjohn's gaze locked on to Stella Rossi. 'Do you want to tell us what really took place that evening, Mrs Rossi?' Stella whispered again to her solicitor. He, in turn, nodded.

'All right,' she said at last. 'We didn't drive to Colloroy because as Michael was out of town, Nigel suggested we spend the evening on one of the yachts at the marina.' Stella Rossi bit her upper lip. 'But we hadn't been there more than a few minutes before Michael climbed down into the cabin.'

'Can you describe what happened, Mrs Rossi?' asked Fitzjohn.

Stella grimaced. 'It was terrible. It really was. Michael started screaming abuse at Nigel and shoved him in the chest. Nigel fell backwards onto one of the bunks. When he managed to get back up, he went for Michael and sent him flying across the cabin. That's when Michael hit his head. On the edge of the sink, I think. It seemed to daze him for a minute or two.' Stella took a tissue from her sleeve and stemmed her tears. 'It was frightening.'

'And then what happened?' asked Fitzjohn.

'Somehow, Michael managed to climb back up on deck. Nigel and I followed, but by the time we got up there, Michael had fallen overboard. He drowned, Chief Inspector.'

'But he didn't, Mrs Rossi. There was no water in Michael Rossi's lungs. He was dead before he entered the water. There was also a second injury to his head. One that he received after he got back up on deck. So, what do you know that you're not telling us?' Stella glared at Fitzjohn in stony silence.

'Withholding evidence isn't going to help your cause, Mrs Rossi, because we'll find out the truth one way or another.' His patience waning, Fitzjohn's glared at her.

Meeting Fitzjohn gaze Stella relented. 'All right. Michael and Nigel struggled again on deck. Michael hit his head a second time.' 'And how did he end up in the water?' Stella did not reply. 'Well?' asked Fitzjohn.

'Nigel pushed him overboard. He said it would look like Michael had slipped down between the pontoon and the yacht when he was coming aboard.'

'And whose idea was it to spring clean both above and below deck?' asked Fitzjohn.

'Nigel's.'

───※───

Fitzjohn and Betts walked into Rossi & Prentice Yachting Electronics, to find Nigel Prentice in conversation with his receptionist. 'Good afternoon, Mr Prentice,' said Fitzjohn. 'I wonder if we can have a few minutes of your time.'

Prentice smiled. 'By all means. Come through, Chief Inspector.' Nigel Prentice led Fitzjohn and Betts into what had once been Michael Rossi's office. He gestured to the chairs in front of his desk as he closed the door.

'It won't be necessary for us to sit down, Mr Prentice,' said Fitzjohn. 'We'd like you to accompany us to Kings Cross Police Station because there have been developments in our investigation into Michael Rossi's death that necessitate we interview you again.'

'Oh.' Prentice looked around. 'Can't we do it here?'

'We'd like to record the interview this time, Mr Prentice,' replied Fitzjohn.

'I see. Well, then... I'll just let my receptionist know that I'll be out of the office for a while.'

⸻

Accompanied by his solicitor, Nigel Prentice sat quietly in the interview room while Betts switched the recording device on and stated the place, date and time. After those present had identified themselves, Fitzjohn, his gaze resting on Prentice, started the interview. 'As I mentioned earlier, Mr Prentice, there have been developments in our investigation that necessitate we speak to you again. It concerns your alibi for the night that your business partner, Michael Rossi, died.' Nigel Prentice's eyes widened. 'A witness has come forward who claims that on the night of Friday, March 17th, you were on Graeme Wyngard's yacht at the time of Mr Rossi's death. Is that true?' Prentice's jaw tightened. 'Well?' asked Fitzjohn. 'Of course, you're not obliged to answer our questions, but I should advise you that it might be to your detriment if you don't.'

Prentice exhaled. 'Okay. We didn't drive to Colloroy that night. Stella wanted to spend the evening on one of the yachts in the marina instead. We'd done so in the past, but this time Mike showed up. He went berserk when he saw me there. I had to defend myself. You do understand, don't you?' Prentice glared at Fitzjohn. 'When I pushed him back, he fell and banged his head on something. There was blood everywhere. I could see he was dazed, but he managed to climb back up on deck.' Prentice took a breath. 'I went up after him. I knew he wasn't steady on his feet. But when I got up there he came at me again. I ducked and he went past me... hit his head again. This time, he didn't get up.' Nigel Prentice closed his eyes. 'I could hear Stella laughing. It was macabre.'

'So how did Michael Rossi come to be in the water?' asked Fitzjohn, his eyes locking on to Prentice.

'It was Stella's idea to put Mike over the side. She said it would look like he'd slipped down between the pontoon and the yacht when he came on board.' Prentice looked down at his hands. 'Stella had planned the whole thing. Phoned Mike and asked him to meet her on the yacht. She knew what his reaction would be when he saw me there.'

Nigel Prentice rested his head in his hands, tears brimming his eyes. 'I didn't want this to happen. I'm so sorry.'

'Caution Mr Prentice, Betts,' said Fitzjohn as he left the room.

⟨CHAPTER 27⟩

Fitzjohn sat back in his chair, his hands clasped together. 'It's been an interesting case, Betts. Our investigation into Michael Rossi's death turned out to be the catalyst for a string of events. More than we could have imagined.'

'And all because of one telephone call,' replied Betts as he emptied the contents of his desk drawers into a cardboard box. 'If Rossi hadn't received the call from Robert Nesbit on that Friday afternoon, he wouldn't have left the winery early, and wouldn't have been in Sydney to meet Stella on Wyngard's yacht that night.'

'True,' said Fitzjohn. 'But if not that night, I think Stella Rossi would have chosen another. I doubt she'd have rested until Michael Rossi was dead. I suspect his infidelity send her over the edge.' Fitzjohn paused. 'She engineered the whole evening with such precision; even to the point of having Nigel Prentice collude with her in murder.'

'You could say Michael Rossi didn't die in vain, sir.' Betts closed his empty desk drawers. 'After all, our investigation into his death has uncovered the real reason for Claudia Rossi's death and revealed her killer, Phillipa Braithwaite.'

'Mmm. He never did accept that his sister's death was accidental, did he? And he was right. But it was more than he could bear to finally be told that Claudia had not only been swindled, but had indeed been murdered. And by her best friend, Phillipa Braithwaite. Of course, Claudia's fate was sealed the moment she started to ask questions about the Brandt sketch. Phillipa Braithwaite would have known that it was only a matter of time before she was exposed as the fraudulent art dealer.'

'What I can't understand, sir, is why Richard Edwards didn't come forward at the Coroner's inquiry instead of waiting until he was on his death bed.'

'Who knows why people do what they do, Betts, but in this case it probably had something to do with the one million dollars he was to receive from the insurance company. He would have been well aware that that wouldn't happen if it was found Claudia had been murdered. And exposing Phillipa Braithwaite as the murderer wasn't going to bring Claudia back.'

'I wonder if he knew for sure that Phillipa had murdered Claudia with the mushrooms,' said Betts.

'I believe he did. I think Claudia would have told him when he returned home from Singapore that Saturday morning in 2010, and found her gravely ill. But he chose to keep it, along with what he knew about the poison pen letters, and the fake Brandt sketch, to himself until he was on his deathbed. The rest we know. Rossi confronted Phillipa that afternoon at the Mosman art gallery. Of course, we'll never know exactly what transpired between them, but I think it caused Phillipa Braithwaite to panic. And when that happened, she made her first mistake by breaking into Esme Timmons's home.'

'Have you heard anything about the money paid out from Claudia's life insurance policy, Betts?' continued Fitzjohn as he sat forward and started to remove the contents of his desk drawers into his briefcase.

'Yes, sir. The MLC has put an injunction on the sale of Richard Edwards's property, and they've also requested the freezing of all his assets until the proceeds of the policy are recovered.'

Fitzjohn closed his briefcase and looked around the Incident Room. 'You know, I've become quite accustomed to this room with its massive amount of space. I'll miss it.' He eyed Betts putting on his suit coat. 'Unlike you, it seems. You look like you're in a hurry to leave, Betts.'

'I am, sir.' A wry smile crossed Betts's face. 'I have a date.'

Fitzjohn's eyes widened, his natural inquisitiveness taking hold. 'And who's the lucky girl?'

'Simone Knowles.'

'Our pathologist? I wouldn't have thought you'd have had time to establish a relationship with all that we've had to cope with over the last couple of weeks. When did you find the time?'

'It wasn't easy, sir. I've been out running, before dawn, with Simone. She's been helping me prepare for the Sydney to Surf Fun Run I'm entered in.'

'But that race doesn't take place until July, does it?'

'No.' Betts grinned. 'I'll see you at Day Street Station in the morning, sir.' As Betts left, Ron Carling appeared in the doorway to find Fitzjohn pulling on his coat.

'Alistair, I'm glad I caught you before you left. You and Martin
Betts have become quite a fixture around here. We're going to
miss you both.'

Fitzjohn's suspicions as to whether Grieg had planted a mole
in Kings Cross Police Station resurfaced as he took Ron Carling's
extended hand. 'Thanks for everything Ron. No doubt our paths
will cross in the not too distant future.'

'They're sure to. And you never know. Chief Superintendent
Grieg might second you here again. Speaking of which, there's
something I want to tell you Alistair. You know the mole you
spoke of the other day? It was me.'

'I thought you might have been. I saw you and Grieg together
in town last week.'

Ron laughed. 'Grieg's idea of a clandestine meeting. I thought
it best to humour the man. He got nothing from me that he could
use against you. But be warned. Grieg's out to destroy your cred-
ibility and your career.'

'I know.' Fitzjohn picked up his briefcase. 'And there's only one
thing stopping him. For the moment at least. I caught him in an
uncompromising position a few months ago.' Fitzjohn thought
back to his chance meeting with Grieg and a woman, other than
Grieg's wife. 'Nevertheless, thanks for the warning.'

Fitzjohn looked out of the side window of the taxi as it pulled
up in front of his cottage that evening to see a soft glow of light
emanating from the front living room window. Puzzled, he paid
the driver and climbed out. As he did so, the front door opened
and Sophie appeared.

'Uncle Alistair. I'm glad you're not late this evening because I've cooked dinner.'

'I didn't expect you to be here, Sophie,' said Fitzjohn, coming through the front gate. 'You said you'd be returning to your lodgings at the university today.' Fitzjohn grabbed the mail from the box.

'That was the plan, but then events took over Uncle Alistair, and you weren't contactable, so I made an executive decision.'

'Oh? What sort of executive decision?' asked Fitzjohn as they made their way through the house and into the kitchen.

'You remember I said that I'd look for a new greenhouse for you?'

'Yes.' Fitzjohn felt an uncharacteristic feeling of apprehension take hold.

'Well, we got the most amazing offer this morning.'

'We did?'

'Yes. A beautiful Victorian style greenhouse. You'll love it, Uncle Alistair. It has everything you could ever wish for in a greenhouse.' Fitzjohn grimaced. 'Staging, shelving, a potting bench. Even automatic vent openers. It's truly the Rolls Royce of greenhouses.'

Fitzjohn put his briefcase on the kitchen table and took his suit coat off. 'And what is this Rolls Royce going to cost *us*, Sophie?'

'Us?'

'You said *we* got an amazing offer so I thought perhaps you might be planning on being a joint owner.'

Sophie frowned. 'No. Not exactly. Not at all, actually. I just didn't want you to miss this great deal.'

Fitzjohn sensed Sophie's euphoria diminish, and he sighed. 'When is it being delivered?'

The smile returned to Sophie's face. 'Oh, you are pleased, aren't you? For a minute there, I thought... Silly of me. It'll be delivered and erected tomorrow morning. And in case you can't be here, I've arranged to stay over for another day.' Sophie beamed.

❧CHAPTER 28❧

In the week following Fitzjohn's return to Day Street Police Station, he arrived at Esme Timmons's home to find an army of landscape gardeners hard at work. From his vantage point on the footpath, he could see Esme settled in one of the wicker chairs on the front porch surveying the activity, and giving the odd direction to her band of workers. She waved when she saw him. Fitzjohn opened the front gate, and dodging between the gardeners and their tools, made his way up the front steps.

'Good morning, Miss Timmons.'

'Morning, Chief Inspector. This is a nice surprise because I didn't expect I'd see you again now that your investigations are complete.' She gestured to the wicker chair next to hers. 'As you can see, I'm having a garden make-over. Claudia loved my garden when it was at its peak, so I decided to have it restored to its former glory.' Esme smiled and her eyes twinkled. 'I didn't get the opportunity to thank you, Chief Inspector, for all you've done for Charlotte and me. I know it can't have been easy. And, as heartbreaking as it is, at least now we know what happened to both Claudia and Michael. And why.'

Fitzjohn smiled. 'I have something here that I think will bring a bit of sunshine, Miss Timmons.' Putting his hand into his pocket, Fitzjohn brought out the Limoges perfume bottle.

'Oh. How wonderful,' said Esme her face lighting up. 'Thank you so much for returning it to me personally, Chief Inspector. I know you're a busy man.' Esme cradled the bottle on her lap and sat quietly for a moment or two. 'You and your Sergeant have been so very kind. I really appreciate it and so does Charlotte.'

'How is Charlotte,' asked Fitzjohn.

'She's feeling much better. She's spending this weekend at Five Oaks. She wanted me to go along too, but I thought it would be best if she went alone.' Esme winked. 'I'm sure that she and Rafe have a lot of catching up to do.'

They sat quietly for a moment or two before Esme said, 'Have you started a new case yet, Chief Inspector?'

'Not yet.'

'Well, when you do, and if you need to discuss it with someone, you can always drop by.' Esme smiled. 'I've been thinking lately that if I had it all to do over again, I'd choose to be a detective rather than a school teacher.'

About the Author

Jill Paterson was born in Yorkshire, UK, and grew up in Adelaide, South Australia before spending 11 years in Ontario, Canada. On returning to Australia, she settled in Canberra.

After doing an Arts Degree at the Australian National University, she worked at the Australian National University's School of Law before spending the next 10 years with the Business Council of Australia and the University of New South Wales (ADFA Campus) in the School of Electrical Engineering.

Jill is the author of three published novels, The Celtic Dagger, Murder At The Rocks, and Once Upon A Lie which are all part of the Fitzjohn Mystery Series. She has also authored two non-fiction books entitled Self Publishing-Pocket Guide and Writing-Painting A Picture With Words.

Also by this Author

The Celtic Dagger

University professor Alex Wearing is found murdered in his study by the Post Graduate Co-coordinator, Vera Trenbath, a nosey interfering busybody. Assigned to the case is Detective Chief Inspector Alistair Fitzjohn. Fitzjohn is a detective from the old guard, whose methodical, painstaking methods are viewed by some as archaic. His relentless pursuit for the killer zeros in on Alex's brother, James, as a key suspect in his investigation.

Compelled to clear himself of suspicion, James starts his own investigation and finds himself immersed in a web of intrigue, ultimately uncovering long hidden secrets about his brother's life that could easily be the very reasons he was murdered.

This gripping tale of murder and suspense winds its way through the university's hallowed halls to emerge into the beautiful, yet unpredictable, Blue Mountain region where more challenges and obstacles await James in his quest to clear himself of suspicion and uncover the truth about his brother.

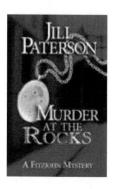

Murder At The Rocks

When Laurence Harford, a prominent businessman and philanthropist is found murdered in the historic Rocks area of Sydney, Detective Chief Inspector Fitzjohn is asked to solve the crime quickly and discreetly. After barely starting his investigation, uncovering a discarded mistress and disgruntled employees, a second killing occurs.

Meanwhile, Laurence's nephew, Nicholas Harford, has his certainties in life shaken when he becomes a suspect in his uncle's death, and receives a mysterious gold locket that starts a chain of events unravelling his family's dark truths.

The Celtic Dagger and Murder At The Rocks, are available in eBook and paperback formats on Amazon. http://www.amazon.com/author/jillpaterson

Connect with me on-line

My Blog
http://www.theperfectplot.blogspot.com

Twitter
http://twitter.com/JillPaterson2

Facebook
http://www.facebook.com/jillpaterson.author

Goodreads
http://www.goodreads.com/author/show/4445926.Jill_Paterson

Official Website
http://www.jillpaterson.com

Amazon
http://www.amazon.com/author/jillpaterson

11879922R00136

Printed in Great Britain
by Amazon.co.uk, Ltd.,
Marston Gate.